The Secret Bunker
Part 1: Darkness Falls

PAUL TEAGUE

SCOTLAND'S SECRET BUNKER

Crown Buildings • Troywood • St Andrews
Fife • KY16 8QH
Tel: 01333-310301 Fax 01333-312040
email: mod@secretbunker.co.uk
web: www.secretbunker.co.uk

GET THE LATEST NEWS ABOUT THE SECRET BUNKER TRILOGY!

More details at http://thesecretbunker.net/book1

ACKNOWLEDGEMENTS

This book was inspired by a family visit to Scotland's Secret Bunker which is located at Troywood in Fife, Scotland, UK, however, it is entirely fictional. If you get the chance, please check out the real 'Secret Bunker', it's an amazing place!

PART ONE: ALONE

Chapter One

In The Beginning

Beyond the great iron doors, I can hear the ghostly wail of sirens. I'm familiar with this noise from school when watching old films about World War 2 and the Blitz. Only this is here and now, and I'm on holiday in Scotland with my family. Surely this must be part of the exhibition? I've never seen Dad so scared. He's terrified and has grabbed Harriet around the waist to get her away from the doors. He's pushing David along at his side. His face is grey - I swear, it's grey. I know from the decisive way he moves that this is no joke, he's genuinely frightened by what's happening outside the bunker.

Standing by the entrance I can see it's overcast and oppressive out there and at first I assume it's just bad weather. But the darkness in the skies has a solid, dark quality. It's like nothing I've ever seen before. As the blackness sweeps through the sky, it shuts out all light. I can't understand what's happening. Even at night there's a glow thrown off by street lamps or passing cars. But this has a finality about it, it's not to be questioned. Suddenly, the heavy iron blast doors, which at first seemed set and fixed, begin to groan and close very slowly. I call out to mum to run faster; they're going to shut before she reaches me.

Dad propels Harriet and David down the long concrete corridor - a combination of pushing and almost throwing them. But this is the action of a man who is the most petrified I've ever seen anybody in my life. It's funny how you notice these things at times like this. In movies, people act alarmed and make all sorts of shouting and screaming sounds. But in real life being scared is a feeling, a terrifying sensation that is played out in silence, inside your head.

As the blackness dominates the sky and casts its deathly shadow over the entrance of the bunker, I call out to Mum as she runs towards the closing doors and I know it must be too late. I hear her calling 'Dan!' but her voice trails off. She's been shut out and we are trapped underground. I have become separated from everybody in the panic. I'm alone in this strange place. Something terrible is happening outside this bunker and mum is caught out there with no way to escape.

April

I can't really remember why we decided to holiday in Scotland. Things have a habit of coming out of nowhere when you live in a big family. One minute Dad has a great idea and then David knocks something over at the dinner table. Dad curses, Mum tells him off (does she really think that we don't hear those words at school?) and Harriet gets covered in whatever it was that just went flying. And, out of the brawl and mayhem that follows, somehow we manage to discuss Dad's great holiday plan, and before you know it he's on his laptop entering the competition.

Yes, this wasn't a conventional holiday for the Tracy family. We couldn't afford a normal holiday. Dad had given up work two years ago, 'Because I'm so old!' he'd joked with us at the time. In actual fact, it was all my fault. I'd had what the teachers referred to as 'difficulties' at school. These 'difficulties' involved hushed conversations among teachers, worried chats long into the night between Mum and Dad, and regular visits from a very unusual man called Doctor Pierce. I remembered him because he wore a brightly coloured tie which had a curious metallic logo embossed on it at the bottom. That struck me as rather strange for a man who was called 'Doctor'. It all ended with me staying at home to be educated.

'Home ed' they called it. Basically it meant that, for me, everything that I'd experienced between the ages of five and fourteen was now over. I got up after Mum had gone to work and, when I did get up, Dad was there. Dad, who'd gone to work before I left the house for ever since I can remember. Usually he was in his pyjamas with a cup of tea at his side and working on something at his laptop. Most days I joined him at the kitchen table about nine o'clock. They let me sleep in later because I lay awake at night. I don't know why that was. I was tired, and I wanted to sleep … but I couldn't. So I was awake until well after midnight usually. I enjoyed the world at that time of night, it was quiet and demanded nothing of me. I love my family, but sometimes, in the middle of the night when the rest of the world is asleep, there is a silence I could inhabit forever.

I preferred home ed because I got to see more of Dad, but I still missed Mum being about during the day. Home ed was funny because very little education took place. I just did what I felt like doing most of the time. And I got along fine like that. All that anger from being at school just seemed to go. In fact, sometimes it was hard to remember what had caused me to get into trouble in the first place. I could remember the rage and the fury – I could recall lashing out at those kids – but I couldn't remember how I'd got from how I am right now to that state where I was so out of control. And I was out of control at school. It's scary to feel that way. But now I feel totally calm, and I can't picture what would make me get that way again. So most of the time during the day it was just me and Dad in the kitchen. And Nat of course, but Nat wasn't actually in the kitchen with us.

When Nat Died

I was thirteen when Nat died. I don't really recollect it as an accident. I remember what people did and how they reacted. And I remember the funeral most of all.

Nat was such great fun and the funeral didn't seem to capture any of that life at all. Mum and Dad remember exactly what happened. I can see it in the sadness when they look at pictures of our family as it was. It comes in an instant, usually when a random photo flashes up on a laptop screen as it switches to screensaver. Then, one minute later, it's almost as if Nat was never in our lives, like that place at the table had always been David's.

But dead people leave a space. It's not a physical space. It's a part of our life that remains in a vacuum. And the smallest thing can let the air rush into that vacuum, filling it with life, memories and feelings, as if the person has never been gone. All it took was a photo and Nat was back at the table with us.

We were twins. I don't think you'd know it now because we weren't identical twins or anything like that. Mum and Dad say 'You were so alike', but we look like two different people to me in those photos.

And if Nat was alive now, I'm sure we'd be so different. For a start, our personalities were opposite. And we wore our hair differently, even at that age. I left mine as it was, Nat was much more adventurous. We were different even then. But always, we were twins – until Nat was killed in an instant by that black car and our lives changed forever.

Chapter Two

Twenty-three Hours After The Darkness Fell

I'm so hungry. I don't think I've ever experienced hunger like this before. At home we always have snacks around. Dad nags us about eating our five-a-day or Mum has a go about ladling too much jam onto our bread. But most of the time, whenever we get peckish, there is food around.

I'm so scared now. I don't know how long I've been here. It's completely dark and there's no sound at all. I don't know where Dad and Harriet are - they were somewhere near David last time I saw them. I've shouted, but there's nothing, just an empty echo from the long concrete corridor. All I have is a half-drunk bottle of water.

If we got lost when we were young, Mum and Dad used to say, 'Find someone with a uniform or wait by the ticket office.' I was by the entrance when the darkness fell. If I had my mobile phone with me I could use the torch on it to see. I've tried feeling my way along the wall, but it's terrifying walking into complete blackness where you can't see anything, not even shapes or outlines. So I did what Mum and Dad said. I waited by the entrance. If anybody comes, that's where they'll go. If only I'd remembered my mobile phone in the car, I'd have some light now. And Mum wouldn't have got caught outside when the darkness came.

Holidays

Somehow we moved from a glass of lemonade getting spilled at the dinner table to a holiday in Scotland. What Dad had been trying to say when this strand of conversation had taken its first breath of life the previous month is, 'Who fancies winning a holiday to Scotland?' Within the mayhem of the spillage, a general consensus of opinion had been reached that Scotland might be a bit of fun and we'd never been there together as a family.

Since Dad had stopped working, money had been tight. It's funny, nobody tells you these things when you're young, you just pick it up from the strands of conversation and what you see going on around you. One minute you're eating your favourite ice cream, the next minute you're stuck with own-brand vanilla flavour. One minute Dad's going to work in a suit, the next minute he's showing you an online video of a funny dog, while he's sitting at the table in pyjama bottoms and a T-shirt with a band's name on that I've never heard of before. Apparently they were great in the 80s.

We used to go on holidays abroad, and we'd all sit and look at the brochures together. We'd fly in planes to places that were far too hot for me and once, we even went on a ferry. Nat loved that ferry …

See – Nat again, always with us but never there.

Losing Nat

I'm not sure if I even saw the black car at the time. In my memory it's there, but I'm uncertain if that's just because I've heard so many people talk about the accident.

I even have a newspaper cutting hidden in my old laptop case upstairs, but I haven't actually looked at it since I put it there. I know that if I look at that faded cutting it will instantly transport me back to the day of the funeral, when that great, empty, immovable void opened before us.

When the final person leaves the house after the funeral, that's when it starts for real. The silence and the coping – that's when it really begins, not when the person dies. There's too much going on after they die, you know they're dead but there's just too much happening. It's only when silence finally descends that you're alone with death. It's only then that you find out how you'll be.

As a thirteen-year-old I never even thought about death. Why would you when you're thirteen? I'm not sure I'd even think about it much now if it wasn't for Nat. Of course, I'd see it in films and cartoons, I'd read about it in books. But that's not really my life and it seems so far away. Always so far away until the final moment of innocence when my twin's blood spattered across my favourite T-shirt and I heard the last gasp for life as Nat's limp body hit the concrete in front of me.

A Lucky Win

So, Dad was entering another competition to win us a

holiday. 'Somebody has to win,' he'd say, 'and it might as well be us!' Then Mum would chime in with some wise catchphrase like, 'You've got to be in it to win it!' Honestly, it was as if they wrote the script before each day started. How did they come up with this stuff, seemingly off the top of their heads?

Usually we entered competitions in magazines or on the back of cereal boxes. Sometimes we even crowded round Dad's laptop to figure out some daft question in an online contest. But I remember this one because it was different from usual. It came via email, directly to Mum.

Now, this is where I should explain that we're a modern family and we all love our tech. Who doesn't? This is the twenty-first century after all! So when Mum got the email, she forwarded it to Dad. 'Hey Mike, I've got some holiday competition from one of my websites, do you want it?'

'Can you forward it to me, Amy?' asked Dad, and after a few taps from Mum on her keyboard I knew that the transaction was complete because five minutes later Dad said, entirely out of the blue, 'Thanks'. The funny thing is, we all knew what he meant by this stray acknowledgement. An onlooker from a hundred years ago would wonder what on Earth had just happened.

This is just how modern families operate - the unspoken fusion of tech and relationships when human interaction can slip seamlessly from words to typing, to reading, and back to words again – and everybody's still in the loop.

Now, Mum was always a deleter. It was virtually the only time that she'd cuss. I think it was because she'd taken on more responsibility in the office since

Dad had stopped going into work and she was sick of emails by the time she was back home. So, about ten minutes after she'd returned from work every night, she'd sit down with a cup of tea, open her laptop, scan her emails, cuss a bit then whack the 'delete' button much harder than was required. 'She's going to wreck that button!' I'd think to myself.

'Sorted!' she'd announce, and then she'd relax and become 'Mum' again, as if deleting those personal emails was revenge for everything she'd had to do at work all day.

That's why I noticed this email in particular. At the time I just assumed that she'd had a better day at work. But now I can see it was something more than that. Anyway, Dad got the email and within seconds of him opening it and asking if we all wanted to go to Scotland we were tapping away at our keyboards trying to find the name of a disused Cold War nuclear bunker in the south of Scotland. David got there first, and he messaged the link to Dad to check it. Dad announced, 'That's the one, never heard of it!' and that was the holiday sorted. Well, almost – until Mum nearly ruined everything by ending up in hospital.

The Empty Ward

The woman sat on the bed with a briefcase at her side. She was browsing something on a digital reader, but it was obvious that she was just distracting herself because when the man entered the room she closed it immediately. She was expecting him and, although she knew him already, she was clearly uneasy about something.

This was a strange place. It had the feel of a

hospital, but it didn't seem to have any patients. There was an antiseptic, clinical feel about it. The beds were neatly made and in rows, but there were no curtains between them, no radios on the walls, nothing extra or decorative.

As the man pressed the pen-like gadget against her neck and the tiny device entered her bloodstream, it struck her that this was almost the same as a military hospital.

A Last-Minute Panic

I didn't even know that Mum gave blood. Not until we got a phone call saying that she'd fainted and they were keeping her in hospital overnight. Dad went into a bit of tirade at that stage. The funny thing about Dad is that he would rant away as if something had bothered him, when it was obvious to everybody in the room that actually he was just very concerned and worried about whoever was involved.

So, while Dad was moaning about Mum's great timing and how it was going to mess up the packing and our early morning departure, me, David and even Harriet really knew that he was just worried sick about Mum. It was that script thing again, as if nobody would finish off his lines if Mum wasn't there.

'I'm going to have to leave you guys here for an hour,' he started. 'Nat, can you look after ...' There it was again. A simple mistake, but Nat was back in the room.

Leaving Nat

Hospitals always meant bad news to me. Of course, in most cases they're places of healing. People who have the most terrible illnesses and problems enter those buildings and most often leave them cured, healed or in greater comfort.

It was the hospital chapel that I particularly noticed when Nat died. I didn't know that hospitals had chapels. My thirteen-year-old self thought that they were made up of wards, lines of beds and filled with doctors and nurses. So much of what we think of these places is from TV and books. A chapel in a hospital makes perfect sense, I know that now.

After all, it's where I first watched my parents crying helplessly as they clung on to each other trying to comprehend that Nat was dead. It was the first and only time in my life that they completely shut me out. It was as if they had to go to each other first before they could come to give me comfort. I know now that the chapel is the most important place in a hospital. It's where people go to pray and beg for help, even if they believe there is no God. It's where people who are ill go when they must come to terms with the end of life. And it's where those who know loss must go, before returning to a home that is missing a child.

Chapter Three

A Late-Night Visitor

Often, as a child, things happen around you and you don't get their meaning. You take them at face value, you see them as they are. One of the things that I had noticed since I'd been at home more was that there was hidden meaning in most things. Take Dad's ranting, for instance. He said one thing, but he meant another. And it was the same with Mum and Dad when they were together. They had conversations, but they sometimes seemed to mean a different thing from what I understood. Like a double conversation, as if the words meant one thing to me, but they were hearing something different.

So, when Dad left me in charge of David and Harriet, he was – on the face of it – going to see Mum after she'd fainted in hospital. But it felt to me as if something else was going on, something I just wasn't getting. Dad wasn't that long as it turned out. I think the reason he was most worried is that Mum had been away the night before. They always got crabby when they didn't see each other for a while. She'd been away at some business meeting and had left to catch an early train long before I got up. Dad was cross that she'd given blood rather than coming straight home. Of course he'd never have known if she hadn't fainted. And now she was in hospital overnight and we were travelling to Scotland the next day.

Sometimes parents seem to make life so difficult. All Dad had to do was get the packing done and pick Mum up from hospital on the way out in the morning. When he got home, David and Harriet went to bed, and Dad got me to help with the packing.

I liked it that since I'd been at home, Dad treated me differently. I couldn't put my finger on it, but it was as if I was an adult at last. He just chatted to me the same as he did with Mum. He didn't use that kind of talk you reserve for kids, as if you're overacting in a bad TV series. That's why I was still up when there was a knock at the door.

It's funny that a knock at the door means nothing at all during the daytime, but at night or in darkness it can take on such a different meaning. At night it can be threatening, or it can take on a new urgency, as if important news has to be delivered that cannot wait until morning. So when the knock came, at shortly after eleven o'clock, it made both of us jump and we could only stare quizzically at each other while we registered what had just happened.

Dad told me to get ready for bed and to stay upstairs, and I felt a sharp change from his easiness in the minutes just before the night-time interruption. I wasn't much the wiser for what was said at the front door – it was just a series of mumbles preceded and followed by greetings and farewells. But there was something about the conversation that registered with me, not words, but a tone and style of speaking. It was only while I was lying awake in bed long after Dad had retired for the night that I finally realized what it was that had felt so familiar to me. That was Doctor Pierce talking to Dad at the door. So why had Dad said, after closing the door and rejoining me, that it was a wrong address?

In The Darkness

I'm trying to stay calm, but it's really difficult. None of this makes sense to me at all. It's as if somebody just turned all the lights out and now they refuse to tell me what's going on. I don't know what to do. If I try to move in this darkness, I might fall. Even worse,

I could get lost.

I'm desperately trying to remember the layout of the bunker beyond the blast doors, but I can't, and anyway it's complete darkness. I have no light or sound to help me navigate. I've called for help until I'm hoarse and my water is gone now. I'm scared, hungry and alone. It's ridiculous, but in spite of this I can think of no better strategy than to stay where I am. If somebody comes, they will either enter via the doors or try to leave using this route.

The thing is, I know there are lots of people still in there. So why can't they hear me? And what happened to Dad, David and Harriet? They were pretty close when the darkness fell, but now I can't see or hear them. It seems crazy to just stay here, but I can't think of anything better to do for now. And if death comes? Well, I was at Nat's side when life ended, so I know what it's like.

Loss

The black car didn't stop when it struck Nat at the roadside. Nobody even thought about the car at the time – everybody's attention was focused on the bloody body that lay lifeless in front of us. It could have been an invisible, brutal force that came out of nowhere and took the life away from my twin without a care. It was only once the ambulance had been called – as Mum cradled Nat in her arms and a crowd of passers-by had gathered – that the question was asked about the driver.

All those people around, yet the only information that we could get about the driver was that he was in a large black vehicle. Make unknown. The driver appeared to be a male. And the car didn't have number plates.

On Our Way

We finally set off on our journey to Scotland. Needless to say, we did win the competition, in the end. We weren't used to having that type of luck, but in this case it was all very quick. It must have been less than a week between Dad sending off our entry and his announcement that we'd actually won, and in no time at all it was the day of the holiday. So, after a chaotic breakfast and a hasty packing of the car, Dad locked up the house, we all got in the car, picked up Mum from the hospital and we were on our way.

Mum seemed fine after her night in hospital. None of us needed any medical detail, so long as Mum was back in sight and we could see her and tell that she was okay, the whole incident was forgotten. Or at least for a while. When I asked her to show me where they'd taken the blood from her arm, there was no mark. 'I must be a quick healer,' Mum had joked. But I didn't think injections healed that fast.

Chapter Four

The Grey Office

She couldn't really feel the device but she knew that it was there. It must have been microscopic to enter her bloodstream so easily and painlessly, and she was uneasy about its presence in her body. But the man was blunt and dismissive – he had the manner of an impatient doctor.

The woman seemed to be wary of him, so held back the questions that she wanted to ask. When he stood up, it was clear that she was supposed to follow him. He took her through a long corridor. This whole building felt military – or governmental at least.

Nothing was there for decoration or pleasure, it was as if things were only around because there was a job to be done. Charmless functionality. She was taken to an office which instantly looked out of place in this building. A nameplate indicated that this was the man's office and it was full of high-tech equipment. Still, the office was grey and without character. The man seemed to have no need to show his personality here. There were no family pictures, no artwork, no attempt to create any life in this room.

This office was like nothing you'd see at home. These were not laptops and screens that you would buy in your high street store. This was something completely different – almost as if they came from a different world.

It was clear that this visit was not yet over for the woman. But in three hours' time she would wake up in her local hospital with no memory of these events. Her husband would be on his way to see her after she'd supposedly passed out when giving blood. That wouldn't feel strange to her at all and she would have no memory of what had taken place earlier. Except there would be a lingering feeling that made her feel uneasy. She wouldn't be able to remember having given blood in the past eighteen years.

The Holiday Highlight

David and Harriet didn't really care what we did on

holiday – they were just happy that we were all together. Mum was not at work and the garden seemed to be a place for great adventures, even in this terrible weather.

As part of the holiday we had a special visit organized. We didn't have to pay for it, but we did have to turn up at an agreed time, so that they were expecting us. Mum and Dad were really excited about it. I wasn't sure what to expect and David and Harriet didn't care anyway. We were going to an old nuclear bunker which lay hidden in the Scottish countryside. According to Mum and Dad, it was a relic from something called the Cold War, when countries didn't get on as well as they do now. From what I could see in the news, countries still didn't get on that well.

Apparently, it was a huge warren of concrete tunnels buried under the ground, the size of a football pitch. At one time it would have been used as a shelter in a nuclear attack. These days, we didn't need it any more.

A Glimpse In The Darkness

I wish I wore a watch because I have no idea how long I've been here now. Never in my life have I known such impenetrable blackness. I used to be scared in my bedroom at night after Nat died, but even then, I could clearly see the objects in my bedroom, though you'd still describe the room as 'dark'.

Something has been bothering me. I've been distracted by fear, hunger and the silence. But I keep thinking back to those last moments before the huge iron doors swung shut. David was right at the end of the long concrete corridor, behind as always. Dad had propelled Harriet along the dimly lit concrete tunnel when he'd seen what was happening outside.

As I stood in the mouth of the doorway, looking up at Mum who was desperately rushing towards the closing doors, I'm sure I saw something else. I'm doubting myself because I know I'm exhausted. But I'm certain she was with a child. The child was my kind of age and height and had a familiar look. Like I'd known them once, but we hadn't seen each other for a while. I'm sure it was Nat.

Chapter Five

The Unusual Holiday

Looking back, the holiday in Scotland was a bit suspicious from day one. But things always seem clearer when you know how they turned out. It's like flicking to the end of a book to see what the ending is. It all seems so obvious when you know how the story finishes – but when you're there, in the thick of real life events, it's not always so clear.

That's how it was with our free holiday to Scotland. I think the fact that we'd won it out of the blue, rather than having to pay for it ourselves, made us much more willing to go along with what they said. After we'd got the 'Congratulations' email, we just took it as a fact we'd won a holiday and we'd soon be on our way.

It's amazing what we accept on the strength of an email. If it looks official, has a nice logo and comes from an address that looks okay, we'll just happily embrace it as we would a phone call or a face-to-face conversation. But many deceptions can lie behind an email, and we're all too willing to be fooled. And so it was with our family.

I think I was probably the only one to notice it, and I can't even remember if I pointed it out to Dad at the time. He called me over to take a look at the email on the morning that it arrived. Mum was at work already, David at school, and Harriet at playgroup. Just me and Dad. It looked just like you'd expect any holiday company email to look. A big banner packed with images of wonderful scenery and happy people. A signature at the bottom of the email that looked as if it was real, but which was really an image. A big, red 'Congratulations' sign at the top of the message. An 0800 'Call us if you have any queries' telephone number in case of problems. Why would anybody be suspicious about that?

Except that company logo was troubling me. Where had I seen something similar to that before? It wasn't a perfect match, mind you, but it was almost as if it had been copied from somewhere.

It took me a day or two before I figured it out. I'm sure that with some problems your mind works away on it in the background and then – at a completely random moment – you just get the answer. My moment of realization came while I was cleaning my teeth with my electric toothbrush, my mind idly skipping from thought to thought. I recalled where I'd seen that logo before. Not exactly the same, but not far off it. It was just like the metallic logo on Doctor Pierce's tie.

I think I saw it more as a coincidence than a clue. With hindsight, it was a very strong clue. To be honest, it was a bit careless, an in-joke that could have given the game away. How many times have you seen something or somebody that reminded you of something else? If one logo looks fairly similar to another, it's not a big deal. Unless you get caught up in the events that we did, of course.

Remembering Nat

Memory is a funny thing. Sometimes I can remember thoughts, events and feelings with absolute precision, as if all five senses captured and recorded every aspect of a particular experience. Other times I wonder if I was even there, my recall is so hazy. Even though I was only thirteen at the time, I can remember certain elements of Nat's accident with remarkable clarity.

Bear in mind that I was processing the world through the eyes of younger child, not a sixteen-year-old. So many of the things that happened, although I didn't fully understand them at the time, have taken on a new significance as I get older.

Three things happened that day that I still remember very clearly. On the day itself, and in the weeks and months that followed Nat's death, these didn't seem to have much significance. But now, when I rerun those events in my mind, things don't seem to quite add up.

It's similar to a complicated jigsaw puzzle. You can know where the corner pieces go, where all the straight edges line up and how colours, lines and shapes need to cluster together to create some sense of the main body. But until that final part slots into place, there is no standing back and seeing what you've got – the picture is incomplete until you have that last piece in place.

There were three pieces of this puzzle that I was unable to slot into place. It was as if they belonged to a different jigsaw. First of all, I'm pretty sure that black car was coming for both me and Nat.

It was only because I stepped back to pick up a coin on the pavement that it missed me. Secondly, Mum had been distracted by somebody talking to her, so she wasn't really paying any attention to what was going on with the traffic.

That's the only reason the car got anywhere near us – Mum's attention was completely elsewhere at the time.

And last of all, I'm pretty certain that I saw Nat moving as the ambulance doors closed and we were parted for the last time.

Inside The Grey Office

Although she would be unable to recall these events, just like those who went before her, the woman was all too aware of what was going on before her memory was erased. To somebody watching from the outside, it would be clear that she was nervous, uneasy, concerned – but she was not being coerced or imprisoned in this room.

She was here of her own free will, but she would rather not be. She'd had to make a choice, and this was the best of a series of bad alternatives. Where there are no good options available, it's amazing how the human mind can make the best of a bad thing. All of a sudden, a choice that in any other situation would look like madness, suddenly becomes the right thing to do. That's how it was for this woman. Whatever the other options that she'd been given, it was better for her to be in this plain office.

It was a sensible thing to have been injected with a tiny electronic device that she didn't understand, by a man she barely knew, in a place she'd never heard of. If this was the best choice, somebody observing these events would be forgiven for asking how bad the alternatives were.

Chapter Six

Connection

I'm not sure if the sirens have stopped or if it's just that the doors to the bunker are so heavy that I can no longer hear them. That last view of Mum running towards the doors is troubling me. That can't have been Nat, I must be imagining it. Anyway, Nat would be completely different now, three years older, just like me. I've certainly changed in the past three years.

I'm much taller for a start, taller than Mum and almost as tall as Dad. This seems to excite Mum and Dad beyond my comprehension. They're always saying things like, 'I'm sure you've grown overnight' or 'You're almost as big as me now'. Personally, I don't really notice, nor do I particularly care. My hair has got darker and I wear it shorter than when I was a kid, too. So, if the positions were reversed, would Nat recognize me now? It would be like one of those photofits that you see on the TV, where they age people who have gone missing. You take a look at the photofit and you can kind of recognize the original person in there. But if you saw them in a crowded place, would you really be able to spot them?

I can't be sure, and anyway, it's ridiculous; Nat

died three years ago, I was there. It must be my mind playing tricks on me, I've been alone in this dark corridor too long. I'm scared, disorientated and exhausted. No, it wasn't the sight of the person that was with Mum that made me think that it was Nat, it was not a visual recognition.

Nat and I were twins and we'd always had a connection. The day I saw Nat carried away in the ambulance, that connection had been broken, like a laptop losing a wireless signal and desperately trying to reconnect. When Nat died, the signal died. I can't be sure who it was outside those doors with Mum. One thing I do know with complete certainty though: when I spotted that person with Mum in the distance, something very strange happened. For the briefest moment, that connection came back online.

Twins

I can't quite remember when I started having 'difficulties' at school. After Nat's funeral, Mum and Dad were keen to get everything back to normal. Of course, there was no 'normal' anymore, not without Nat. It hit me hardest I think. I may be wrong, but seen through my thirteen-year-old eyes, everybody else seemed to adjust quite quickly.

I suppose you can't cry all the time; at some point, you have to get back to the things that you did before the death. Even though you carry that empty feeling inside you. I knew Mum and Dad were sad, but it was hidden by the routines of daily life. Piling dirty washing into the machine. Putting the used plates into the dishwasher. Cutting the grass and weeding the flower beds. Trivial, stupid things force grief aside and demand to be done. And so it was in our house.

But I was struggling. I can only describe it as 'searching for a signal'. That's how it felt without Nat. When Nat had been around I'd been fine, I felt perfectly okay. But when Nat died, I was left searching desperately for something that wasn't there anymore.

I know all twins will tell you that. They're incredibly close, they sometimes know what the other twin is thinking and feeling. Amazing how humans work. But this was different, it wasn't just about closeness. I didn't have the words to explain it at the time. Now I do. It really was as if we were fused in some way, locked together, dependent. 'Symbiotic' is the word I found in the online dictionary, it describes it perfectly. And so when Nat died, it wasn't so much one death, it was more like two.

Trouble At School

I had real trouble adjusting to life without Nat. They handled me with kid gloves at school. Or at least for a while they did. Just like washing plates and cutting grass, real life has a habit of getting in the way. In a class of twenty teenagers, there was only so long I had to get over Nat. The reality was that they needed me fully functioning as soon as possible, there's only so long that you can put up with a problem child in a busy classroom. So all the time, I felt as if I was desperately trying to re-establish this connection.

It wasn't just sadness, loss and grief. I couldn't articulate it at the time, and I just thought it was what everybody else in the family was going through too. To be honest, I didn't cope with it very well at all.

Sometimes it would drive me mad. I just needed to get that connection back with Nat and I'd be fine. So, if other kids caught me at the wrong time, I'd just go crazy with them. A bit of stupid teasing, some playful pushing, a daft comment. Sometimes, when I was struggling with my 'disconnection' with Nat, I would just lash out.

Before I knew it, the hushed conversations had begun. Mum and Dad were being called in after school to chat with my class teacher. When it gets really serious, the head teacher is involved and Mum and Dad are having those conversations during the working day. And before you know it, you're being introduced to a man with an unusual tie, called Doctor Pierce.

The Holiday Itinerary

I wasn't unusually troubled by that logo at the time because I was more interested in the details of the holiday. It made no difference to me, of course, but this holiday had to be taken in term time. That was okay for us, because Harriet could skip nursery and David would be able to come out of school for a week. Mum and Dad had pulled this one off before, and so long as you called it an 'educational visit' and made a big thing of the incredible learning experiences involved, the head teacher usually let you get away with it. Mum and Dad didn't bother mentioning the long morning lie-ins, the evening DVDs and the trips to our favourite burger restaurant. Always best to miss those bits out when talking to the head teacher.

We seemed to be pretty free to do as we pleased

for most of the time. But they were very insistent about that trip to the bunker. In fact, although it was written in a really cheery way, it was made pretty clear that if we didn't make that bunker visit, there would be a 'penalty' to pay. I scanned words like 'publicity opportunity', 'sponsor involvement' and 'extra spending money' – enough to know that if there was one thing that had to happen on this holiday, it was getting to that bunker at the appointed time.

Chapter Seven

Jigsaw

There were three pieces that didn't quite fit in this jigsaw. Yes, they were part of the overall picture, but they felt as if they'd been taken out of another set. Why do I remember Nat moving, for instance? That image doesn't belong in this picture. Nat died, I was there at the funeral. It was the way it happened that made me remember it. I know now that when people die it's not like it usually happens on TV. It can be slower than that in real life, it takes more time. It's actually quite hard for people to die, in fact, particularly if you're trying to kill them.

People die of all sorts of crazy things every day – such as slipping on ice, choking on toast and even laughing themselves to death. But to purposefully kill them is quite hard. It's all there on the internet, people die of silly things. I did say that home education is nothing like school. I have plenty of time to research this stuff. So, it was perfectly possible that Nat could have moved after being hit by the black car. Again, my source was the internet, so I hope it's correct, but it was on a reputable site.

After death occurs, there's a period called 'clinical death' where a person can be revived. Well, Nat was pronounced dead at the scene of the accident, even though the body was still taken away in the ambulance. The blood on my clothes was certainly for real and Nat was completely still in the road as the medical staff scurried around the body, doing their best to save another life. I don't really know what death looks like, but even to my thirteen-year-old self, Nat looked dead to me. But probably only a thirteen-year-old would have seen this.

The adults were all talking and busy. Mum was being comforted by a police officer and I was chatting to an ambulance man, close enough to see what was going on.

From nowhere, a man joined the huddle of medical staff around Nat's body. He showed them some sort of card, I'm guessing that it must have been identification. Whatever it was, they jumped at it and it was obvious even to me that he was now in charge.

As they started to move away from the body, and in the second that they were distracted, and thrown off balance by the arrival of this man, he did something to Nat. I couldn't see what it was – it wasn't an injection, but whatever he did had the same motion as giving somebody an injection. Nat's body didn't do anything immediately, in fact I only saw the movement just as it was being lifted into the ambulance.

It could have been anything, of course. I have no knowledge of medical procedures and he certainly looked as if he knew what he was doing. It was just very surprising that this man had been the same person who had distracted Mum immediately before Nat's accident.

Meeting Doctor Pierce

When you're a kid, you're introduced to all sorts of adults and people in authority and you're expected to just accept it as a normal part of life. Yet, at school, at home and even in TV programmes, you're warned constantly about 'stranger danger'. What's a kid supposed to think, for goodness' sake? One minute I'm being told that I have to see this doctor who I really don't like, then next minute I'm being told to alert a responsible adult if someone talks to me and it makes me feel uncomfortable. Well, that's exactly how Doctor Pierce made me feel. In fact 'uncomfortable' wasn't the word for it.

It wasn't because I was frightened of him or anything like that. He just had real problems communicating with children. He was so intelligent and high flying, that I really struggled to relate to him.

And that tie of his, what was that all about? I never really listened to what he was saying, because I was watching that tie all the time. The metallic quality of that logo was really unusual. Metallic objects usually catch the light and often reflect different colours based on the surroundings. Only Doctor Pierce's tie didn't do that.

The metallic logo on his tie seemed to have a life of its own and reflected colours that weren't even in the room.

Or at least I'd noticed that whenever I was anywhere near him, that's what happened.

The Day Of The Visit

It was pretty amusing on the day of the visit to the bunker. In fact, if I never saw my family again – and I had to consider that possibility at the time – it was a pretty nice 'final day' together.

Mum was so funny. She got a real bee in her bonnet about us being tidy if the holiday people were going to take a publicity photograph of us all. Dad was a bit stressed too. We all knew money was tight, but that extra spending money that we were due to pick up … well, anybody would have thought it was the Holy Grail that we were collecting.

Dad was determined to get there on time and bank that extra cash. It was one of those scenes of family chaos, where Mum's trying to get us all decent and ready at a certain time, Harriet's rebelling by spilling juice all over herself five minutes before we go out and Dad's doing a big 'countdown to leaving the house' to make sure none of us gets distracted by our tech.

The only problem is, we didn't have an internet connection in this holiday house. Can you believe that? Who doesn't have a broadband connection these days? Well apparently, some rural areas in Southern Scotland don't. Give me city life any day. So it's fair to say that we were all pretty desperate to get connected. And they had free wireless at the bunker. Thank goodness, civilization at last.

Mum and Dad refused to take all of our tech, they were too embarrassed, so the deal was – as we were 'guests' on this visit – that we'd just take Mum's laptop and my phone and have five minutes 'catch-up' time in the café.

That's why Mum got caught outside the doors when the darkness came. It was 'tech-time' and we had left my phone and Mum's laptop in the car.

Calibration

The woman was sitting uneasily on the low, hessian-covered chair. It was a small concession to comfort, though they both knew that comfort was not going to be a primary concern in what happened next. The doctor moved over to the computer equipment and began to make hand gestures on the screen.

This was advanced technology, recognizable for what it was – screens, speakers, camera, tech hubs – yet somehow unfamiliar.

As the doctor moved his hands, there was a faint, pulsing glow just beneath the skin on the woman's neck. It was where the device had entered her body only minutes before.

Whatever it was, it was receiving some signal from the equipment in that room. She could barely feel it; it brought no pain or discomfort, but she knew that something was going on.

The doctor never spoke to her while all of this was happening. He didn't offer words of reassurance or explanation as you might expect from a medical professional.

The woman had experienced all different types of doctor in her lifetime – friendly, brash, superior, calming – but never one like this.

This man made no effort to establish a rapport or demonstrate an appropriate bedside manner.

If she had to describe how he made her feel, she'd probably say, 'Uncomfortable'.

Chapter Eight

Underground

After all the mayhem, we did actually get to the bunker in time. At first, we were really disappointed. When Mum and Dad had been talking about 'Cold War bunkers' and 'nuclear proliferation' I'd conjured up all sorts of images of an imposing military base surrounded by barbed wire and missiles. Okay, I knew this was disused and now a visitor attraction, but it just had the appearance of a boring cottage from the outside, with a few suggestions of possible military use as you drove up to the car park.

I don't know what it is about government buildings, but they very definitely have a 'look' and a 'feel' about them. They're well-built, strong and robust. They're also businesslike, functional and plain. That's how I'd describe the cottage. For all intents and purposes it was a regular cottage. But the guttering was metal, not plastic; the fence posts were concrete and nothing was done for decoration, it was purely functional. The land surrounding the cottage was scattered with man-made knolls, some of which had aerials and dishes perched on them, others looked like ventilation outlets and the rest were just concrete stores. It was a rural and hilly area, with a mobile-phone mast close by and lines of pylons dotted along the horizon.

It became immediately clear from a map just outside the main entrance that this was just the shop and ticket-buying area, the real Secret Bunker was concealed deep beneath the ground.

Our sheer excitement at the adventure that awaited

us beyond the ticket desk distracted us from the fact that our hosts had not turned up. There was a message waiting for us as we were handed our free tickets, apologizing for the delay and asking us to go ahead and look around the bunker. We'd be joined in the café in about one hour's time. By somebody with the surname Pierce.

A Sudden Sound

My anxiety has taken over again and I'm not really thinking now about what happened just before I lost sight of Mum. I'm really hungry and considering making my way along the corridor again. I've tried calling out to Dad, but my cries are just returned to me as an echo. Why can't they hear me? They weren't that far away. And what the devil is going on out there?

Mum was caught outside the closing blast doors, there's no way she can get through those. The sign outside said that they weigh three tonnes. When the alarms sounded, they closed automatically.

Funny that: they looked as if they'd be manually operated, they had handles on them the same as the ones that you see in submarines, the type that you have to turn several times to open and close. I don't think I'd be able to hear her through them, either.

I thought that most places had emergency lights when something unusual like this happened. I suppose this place is just a museum now, but still, we're so deep underground, why didn't the lights come on? My mind starts to race again with all the different scenarios and possibilities. The simple fact is, I just don't know what's going on. I tried to get up and walk along the corridor one more time, but I just gave up again. It's so dark, if only I could hear somebody or something, I'd have a destination to aim for. I'm pretty sure that if I can't hear Dad, he must have made it past the next set of doors, so all I'm going to reach is a dead end if I move forward.

And then I'm startled, because out of the silence and blackness, I can hear a noise. It's not a person, there is no voice or movement. It is the faint hum of something that sounds electrical, as if somebody just turned the power on.

The Other Pieces

Three years on, and I was still pretty sure of what I saw. But as a thirteen-year-old child you receive the world as it's presented to you by adults. Nat was dead, Mum and Dad were distraught and there was a funeral. It must be so. Only I knew what I'd seen. I couldn't explain it, but I knew that it had happened.

And what about that man who'd distracted Mum? Was it a coincidence that he was there at that time? In films, if somebody has a heart attack on a plane, they always ask for a doctor. There's usually one on board. So was this just a happy coincidence?

As a thirteen-year-old I was unsure. My sixteen-year-old self was definite that it was no coincidence. And there was one thing that I knew with complete certainty about that day. Again, it was a feeling in the moment, an instant of understanding, vision and acceptance. As I stepped forward with Nat, then stepped back to take a look at that coin on the ground, I looked up. A black car was coming at us at speed, Nat just hadn't seen it. In that moment I looked up and saw the eyes of the driver. This was no driver error, no careless steering or momentary lapse of concentration. He was looking at me directly in the eyes and the car was being aimed straight at us.

Chapter Nine

Concealed

The Secret Bunker was amazing. I was at that age where I could often take or leave Mum and Dad's family days out, but this one captivated the entire family.

There was nothing ornate or subtle about the place. It was a massive concrete bunker buried one hundred feet under the ground. You reached it via a 450-feet sloping tunnel, accessed through the cottage. The bunker itself was incredible. There were offices, control rooms, dormitories and bathrooms. There was a chapel and even a radio studio. I hadn't a clue why anybody would want to hear a DJ playing tunes after a nuclear apocalypse, but Dad informed me that radio would be used to transmit important messages from the Government in the event of an emergency. I think I'd prefer the DJ.

We found what must have been a mini cinema on our explorations, and inside they were showing Cold War films in black and white. Part of me wanted to laugh at these films, another part of me knew how deadly serious they were. They were explaining what to do in case of a nuclear attack. Men with really posh voices used phrases such as 'Duck and cover' and 'Protect and survive' and you'd see old-fashioned school children practising what to do when the bomb went off. It only struck me looking back how ominous the sound of the sirens had been in those old films.

Twenty-four Hours After The Darkness

It's only a faint hum at first, and I can feel it as much as see it, because with the noise comes a small vibration through the floor. Whatever is creating this must be pretty big and powerful – or extremely close – as I'm feeling it through a thick wall of concrete. It is building slowly, and it doesn't feel to me like a generator, it's not a sound I've ever heard before.

Still this wretched darkness though, I'd had a sudden leap of hope when the humming had started, expecting the lights to come on and everything to be resolved. What I'd give for this all to be sorted. In an instant, the humming alters pitch, as if somebody just changed the gears of a car. It has an urgency now and I get the sensation for the first time in however many hours it has been that something is changing around me, but I can't quite put my finger on it.

The lights come on. I am dazzled and confused for a moment, my eyes are used to the blackness and I'm now immersed in bright light. As my eyes struggle to adjust, I look up to see that I am no longer where I thought I was. This is still the long corridor, but it has somehow been transformed since I last saw it.

I don't have time to question that. Three figures wearing virus-protection suits are running towards me and, as they do so, the small, red lights from the laser targeting on their weapons come to rest in unison on my forehead.

PART TWO: DISCONNECTED

Chapter One

Revelation

I have never had a single gun pointed directly at me before – let alone three – and it's not something that I'd recommend. On TV, people wave guns around as if they're toys. Right now, it's pretty terrifying having these three red dots directly above my eyes and knowing that at any second – should a trigger be pulled – it's all over for me. These aren't regular guns though, they're certainly weapons and they're definitely modelled on guns. They belong to a science fiction world rather than the twenty-first century.

It doesn't help that these guys are dressed in virus suits. I'm no expert, but I know that can't be a good thing for me. They're completely sealed off in these suits from head to toe. The suits are bright yellow, there's no missing them, that's for sure. As the three figures get closer I can see that I'm being approached by two women and a man, each looking deadly serious, intent but concerned. That's a considerable improvement on hostile, but I'd still rather those laser dots were not trained directly on me. And what's happened to this corridor?

Before the doors closed and the lights went out, this was just a gloomy, concrete-lined passageway. Was I unconscious for a while? Did I fall asleep? Did somebody move me? No, I can tell that this is the same place, the same long corridor, but before the lights went on, it completely changed. It's as if a team from one of those TV decorating programmes popped in while the lights were off and gave the corridor a total makeover. Only this looks like nothing I've ever seen before. Let's put it this way, it belongs more to the realms of imagination and fantasy than a Cold War bunker in Southern Scotland.

Either I passed out for a while, or this is what I thought was the vibration of the power coming back on. What I believed to be movement in the building must have been this internal transformation taking place. It's quite incredible. Gone are the grubby, cold, concrete walls; they've now been replaced by some light, plastic or metallic, substance. If I had to describe it, I'd say it looked just like the interior of a space station. Not that I've ever seen one, mind you, but it's what I'd imagine one would look like.

I should have concentrated on the three figures approaching me. One of the women has pressed the trigger on her weapon, a ray of some kind strikes my head and my thoughts stop dead.

The Missing Host

Needless to say, the Tracy family visit to the bunker was a huge success. I've seen it on adverts many times, but in this case the slogan was true. There really was 'something for everyone' here.

The scale of the bunker was astonishing. Rooms and corridors the size of a football pitch over two levels is quite some feat. When you're walking along that rabbit warren of passageways – with no natural light – you understand what an amazing structure this is. And how much concrete they must have used. They certainly won't have mixed that all by hand.

Had there been a nuclear attack, life could have continued here virtually as normal. Everybody would have had a job, of course, and the Control Room was where all activity would have been focused. We had a good hour looking around until Mum reminded us that we were due to meet our hosts in the café area on the top level. We'd been shushed quite a lot as we walked around the bunker.

Harriet and David loved the lengths of the corridors, and had used that as an opportunity to go running off into the distance, then charging back at Mum and Dad. I couldn't be completely certain about this, but I'm pretty sure that I sensed a hostility from the other adults who were in the building. I didn't know why, as this was a tourist attraction, it's not as if we were in a church or someone's office or anything like that. But I did wonder why were there no other children there except for us.

The Jigsaw Puzzle

The black car had been driving directly at us. There's no mistaking something like that. I was equally sure that I had seen Nat moving. And I knew that Mum had been distracted by that man, the one who went to help Nat. Was he helping Nat? The ambulance workers accepted his authority, they knew exactly who he was. Or maybe they didn't know him, but they understood and acknowledged his position. There was no challenge or argument from them, no resistance at all.

Three parts of a jigsaw puzzle that didn't quite fit. As if they belonged somewhere else, pieces of another puzzle. I'd been troubled by this for three years now. But when you know that your twin is dead, when you've learned to accept that, because all the evidence confirms it, there's not much that you can do about it.

Unresolved issues never go away. As humans, we need closure, we can't just forget things. Life would be much easier if we could, and just delete a section of our memory that is no longer required or wanted. So although I couldn't do anything about them, these memories troubled me.

But in the events that followed in the Secret Bunker, I was going to get all the answers I needed.

Chapter Two

Revival

I don't recall anything between the weapon going off and waking up in the medical area. I'm not even certain as to how long I was out – asleep, knocked out, unconscious or whatever it was – but it must have at least been overnight because I feel pretty well rested after the gruelling events that I've experienced alone in that corridor. It doesn't hurt, so that's a relief. Whatever those weapons were, they weren't there to hurt me. I'm not even sure if they were weapons now – seeing that I'm here, healthy and unhurt.

My mind is feeling a little fuzzy, no worse than having to wake up on any other day, mind you, but it quickly accelerates from zero to one hundred miles per hour. So many questions ... what's going on here? What happened to the bunker? Who were those people who came out to get me in the corridor? Why were they wearing virus suits? But most important of all, where is my family?

The room is well lit and extremely modern. It's more hi-tech than anything I've seen before. This is a room for medical purposes, but it doesn't look or feel anything like a hospital. There are data screens everywhere, similar to computers, yet not like anything I've ever seen in a regular hospital.

There is no sinister, metal, torture-like medical equipment set out on trays and I can't see any containers or medicines. And there are no syringes anywhere, which is always a good thing. Everything in this room seems to happen electronically. I am alone, but I see that I am being monitored on a camera which is pointing directly at me.

I am comfortable, warm and not in any immediate danger, so in spite of all my questions, I can only assume that whatever is going on is not a threat to me. I also hope that it means Dad, Harriet and David must be on the receiving end of the same treatment. I'm desperate to see them, but it doesn't appear as if that's going to happen at the moment.

And what about Mum? If those guys came out into the corridor in virus-protection clothing, what the heck is going on beyond the bunker doors? And what does that mean for Mum who's currently trapped outside?

Waiting

At the time, I'd assumed that there were no other children in the bunker because we were here during term time. But that only excluded families with school-age children. What about those with toddlers? It's very unusual not to see any other children. But that wasn't the only thing.

There didn't seem to be any couples in the bunker. There were men and women of different ages, but none of them seemed to be together. It was as if it was an open day for childless and friendless people. There were plenty of people visiting the bunker; I'd even go as far to say that it was quite busy.

But none of them seemed connected – and here's the other thing that struck me. Most of them weren't engaged in the exhibits in the same way that we were. It was almost as if they were just hanging around waiting for something to happen.

Control Room

The terminal was active now, and all was as it had been during the training. The location was different of course, much more modern than that grey and functional building. But this was exactly how they said it would be. He'd trained alone, in isolation. There were no colleagues to laugh and joke with, it was important that each person knew their role completely.

His workstation was an exact replica of what he'd had at the Orientation Centre. Everything exactly the same, including the framed photograph of his family. He'd been trained thoroughly and precisely, so he knew exactly what to do and when to do it. He understood that his instructions would arrive at the appointed time.

All was as it should be, except for the long delay activating the lighting. But he couldn't help worrying about Trudie and the kids. They said that his family would be okay on the outside. It would only be for a limited time, they said. And he didn't really have a choice. 'No families!' was the strict policy on this mission. So long as they were in their home when the darkness fell, they'd be okay.

Outside

The darkness began at 15:00 BST on 15 May. It was undetectable at first. Just like the weather had changed and the skies were going grey. Only this was a weather pattern that was occurring everywhere. It had been preceded by high winds and extreme atmospheric conditions.

It was the sort of weather that grounds planes and stops ships setting off to sea. This was a global phenomenon. The same forecast would have covered the entire world. It appeared that somebody wanted as much of the world as possible locked up safely at home.

Chapter Three

Kate

While I'm thinking about Mum and what might have happened to her, a screen in front of my bed jumps into life and positions itself directly in my view. At a perfect focal distance. Very clever. A face appears on the screen.

'Hello Dan,' says a very official looking lady on the screen, 'I'm sorry if we worried you.'

'That's fine,' I reply. 'But what's going on? And where is my family?'

'Sorry Dan, there's a lot to explain,' she continues. 'Would you prefer to get some food first, then I can brief you fully on what's been happening?'

I'm really hungry and I'm never very good on an

empty stomach. The thought of sitting down with a plate of decent food and getting some answers is just what I need right now. But I want to know about my family first.

'Where is Dad?' I ask. 'He must be here with David and Harriet still. Is this the same bunker or have I been moved?'

'Dan, your dad and your brother and sister are fine, but I'm afraid we can't let you see them just yet,' replies the lady. 'You're in a classified military area; we have to follow certain protocols, I'm afraid,' she continues. 'But let me reassure you, they're absolutely fine.'

'And my mum?' I ask, relieved that at least I seem to be safe now, and things are looking more hopeful by the minute.

The face on the screen changes slightly. She tries to hide it, but I can see that she is suddenly concerned. I have caught her out; she wasn't expecting that question.

'Dan, were you with somebody else when you got caught in the bunker? Other than your brother and sister, and your dad?'

'Yes,' I reply. 'My mum.' I'm concerned now; I don't like the look on her face. She's referring to somebody off-screen, as if she hopes that they'll give her an answer. This doesn't feel like it's going to be good news.

'Dan, there was nobody else inside the bunker when the doors closed, where was she?' the woman asks me uneasily.

'She was outside,' I reply, 'running towards the blast doors.'

'Oh,' is the only word that she utters.

Recruited

He was pretty surprised when the recruitment call came. He was ex-military. Struggling to return to civilian life. It's a big change when you leave the Army. One minute you're in a foreign country being shot at, verbally abused and fearing for your own life and the lives of your colleagues. The next you've been made redundant and your military life is over. The routines, the discipline, the friendship. It takes some adjusting to.

It had only been three weeks when the call came, but he was ready for it. A few trips to the job centre and he'd known that civilian life was going to be a struggle. How can you be a waiter in a pizza restaurant when only a few weeks ago you were dodging sniper bullets and trying not to step on a landmine? So he was eager to get involved when they contacted him.

It was almost as if they'd been waiting. When they asked him to sign up, he was desperate to get back in action, there was no way he was saying 'no'. Trudie would understand. And at least nobody would be in danger. Or that's certainly how it had looked at the time.

Anticipation

'Uncomfortable' is not a good word to use to describe the person who's responsible for medical procedures, especially if they involve you and your body.

But the woman had not really had a choice. When they put it the way they did, what else could she do? If it was your family, wouldn't you be able to make tough decisions if it meant them being okay? And this didn't seem too bad, it certainly hadn't hurt at all. She'd had more discomfort from a filling at the dentist. Only once you'd had a filling it was all over and done with. And if you went easy on the sweets and drinks, you could even avoid it happening again if you really wanted to.

But she had a feeling that sitting here in this office, having this thing – whatever it was – placed into her body ... she had a feeling that this was the easy bit.

Orb

Although the darkness had the appearance of an accelerated nightfall at first, if viewed from space, it would have looked much more startling. This had nothing to do with the sun, or the light that is cast over the planet, depending on where you are in the world, at certain times of day. This blackness fell over the entire planet.

From space you would have seen no land, no sea, no mountains or clouds. You would just have observed those familiar forms slowly darkening, until completely obscured by blackness. Nothing – just an orb of darkness – and no signs of life.

Chapter Four

Normality

The woman is called Kate and although I can't get over my concern about Mum – and my eagerness to see Dad, Harriet and David – I like her and I feel safe in her company. It's the security of being with someone who knows what's going on. It seems to be my best bet at the moment. I have so many questions to ask, but I'm trying to stay calm and sensible. I know that if it all comes pouring out the way I'd like it to, we'll get nowhere.

I want to ask a thousand questions at once and get all the answers right now. Unfortunately, I know that won't happen. Also, there's a sense of urgency in this building. Nobody is saying anything; there are no alert signs or anything like that. It's just the way that people are getting on with their work: they've been trained for this and they know exactly what they're doing.

And here's another funny thing: all of these people were in the bunker when we were visiting as a family. They are the same people who appeared to be surprised at our presence there. Twenty-four hours earlier they had seemed to be in the wrong place. Now it is quite clear that they were all in the bunker for the same reason. They have jobs to do here. I'm not even sure that they knew each other before this all happened. They're working together, but there is no easy chat or sense of familiarity. They seem bound now by a common sense of purpose, by work and activities that they all understand. They have all been trained for this. They were expecting it to happen.

The Military Approach

He looked at the picture of Trudie and the kids, then placed it to one side. As a military man, he knew how this worked. Focus on the job and get through it. He'd been away from the family for six months at a time before. They were used to it. They didn't like it, of course. Who would? So one month away from home – and in the same country? Well that was a luxury compared to a tour of duty. The training had been military in nature, even though he knew it wasn't Army.

It was probably safer to say that it was a 'government' job. But the routines were the same as the Army. The Official Secrets Act and all that. They wanted ex-military people because of the way they'd been trained. This was not a civilian job, it needed military discipline and routines. The biggest difference was that you weren't a unit. In fact, he hadn't met anybody connected with this mission yet.

First it was the training. In isolation. He'd felt bad about lying to Trudie, but she knew the score.

It was no different to having to keep quiet about military operations abroad. Every part of him wanted to share this stuff with her, after all they were husband and wife weren't they? But he'd just told her he'd had to go away for a week to an assessment centre for a new job. She didn't ask too many questions. Just the obvious 'Where is it?', 'Who is it with?' and 'How long are you away?' She was used to being on her own with the kids, it would just be the same as life in the Army again. Only without the constant worry and the fear that there might be a knock at the door from someone bearing bad news.

The training had been just like old times for him. A functional government building, a purposeful regime and perfunctory relationships with your superiors. Except for that doctor who seemed to be in charge. This man certainly knew his stuff when it came to the tech they were using. But he was an 'odd one'. He'd really felt uncomfortable whenever this guy was around.

He missed the laughs with his colleagues though. He knew he'd be joining other people for the main operation, but they would not meet before the event. They were to be trained in isolation, via simulations, so that each person knew exactly what to do when all the elements were placed together. This was quite different from military training where they acted as a unit, under central command. It was almost as if no single person was supposed to know exactly what was going on.

Activation Process

If this was the easy bit, she might as well relax and get on with it. She'd had enough experience at work to know that you should take one thing at a time. No point worrying about what might happen next week. Focus on what's going on now. Whatever was going on with those screens, it was obviously connected with this thing inside her. They wouldn't tell her what it was, only that it was 'mission critical' and non-permanent. How reassuring. When he talked about 'mission' she hadn't a clue what it was. Only that she had no choice but to get involved and to play her part.

It was similar to her short stint in the Army before she met Mike. Following orders, doing what you're told, never asking questions. It hadn't really worked out for her then so it was almost a relief when redundancy came. It was one of the shortest military careers in history. Long enough to get a feel for it, not long enough to see any real action. Except for the one mission of course. The one that changed everything.

She wasn't really the 'trusting authority' type. Look at how they'd home educated Dan. Most people don't even know that's possible. They just follow the rules, do what everybody else does. And taking David out of school during term time. Okay, these weren't the crimes of the century. But she had a natural aversion to doing what she was told. Except when the lives of her family were being threatened.

Relays

Satellites were relaying these images back to Earth, but there was no one awake to see them.

They were appearing on PC screens, but nobody was able to look at them.

If they could have seen them, they would have wondered how this could have happened. An entire planet plunged into darkness.

The light of the sun was making no impact on that blackness whatsoever, the whole planet had the appearance of being encrusted in a solid, black shroud.

The light just shone behind it, similar to a full eclipse. It looked so still and calm from space, but on the planet surface, Hell had just been let loose.

Chapter Five

Familiarity

I get a really strange sensation as I walk through the bunker. I can recall enough of my tour over forty hours earlier to know that the basic shape and layout has been preserved.

For instance, when I exit the medical area, I can tell that it is in the same position as it was earlier, because the chapel is directly opposite as I step outside.

Everything is exactly where it should be. But it's like a scene change in a play. As if somebody came on stage while we weren't looking and made the place look completely different. It's so modern and high-tech now.

If you'd taken the basic concept of the original Cold War bunker, redesigned it for 200 years in the future, that's what I'm looking at now. It's light and bright, the air is fresh and dry, and all of the old-fashioned equipment, posters, wiring, pipework and paintwork has gone.

Whatever happened here, it is like no technology that I recognize. And believe me, I know my tech! It has literally transformed the inside of the bunker, but it did so without a single builder, plumber or electrician. Which is probably a good thing if the ones we use at home are anything to go by.

Kate and I are now sitting in what was previously – only hours earlier – a fairly basic café. It was where we were supposed to have met our hosts, though we never made it in the end. Neither did they, come to think about it. We'd been on our way, when David and I remembered the laptop deal that we'd done with Mum and Dad earlier. Five minutes each on Mum's laptop using the free wireless connection in the café.

So instead of making directly for the café, Mum had left us all near the entrance with Dad, while she headed back to the car to grab the laptop. And my phone, I'd left that in the back of the car, too. If we were near the entrance, we'd see our hosts when they entered the bunker, so that seemed like a pretty good strategy at the time.

She'd only been gone a few minutes when the sirens sounded. At first we thought it was just something to do with the Secret Bunker. A bit of novelty for the tourists perhaps. But it was very obvious that this was for real. The sirens were outside, for starters. Previously we'd just heard them on the Cold War films that were showing in the cinema area. Red lights were flashing throughout the corridors too. And the announcement system gave it away as well: 'All personnel operational. This is not a drill.' That's when Dad knew it was for real, at about the same time as the bunker doors began to close. It's when he tried to take us deeper into the building. It must have been instinctive, whatever was going on outside, this bunker could offer protection. And that's when I last saw Mum. And that terrible blackness outside. What was that? I know the Scottish weather can be bad at times, but this was much more than just a terrible storm.

There are a lot of things happening like that at the moment. So sitting with Kate now is an opportunity to get things straight. The café before the darkness had been decorated 'Cold War' style. This is still basic and functional – it isn't a fancy restaurant or anything like that – but it is a lot fresher and much more modern. And the food looks great. So I sit down with Kate, tuck into my food and wait for her to begin.

Forgotten

The process, whatever it was, seemed to be over. The

doctor had made a few final brisk swishes of his hands across the screens and they shut down. His manner told her that this was not the time to be asking questions. Particularly questions such as 'What happens next?' or 'How will I know when it's time?' Besides, she wouldn't remember any of this until the device was reactivated.

The doctor moved to another console on his desk, tapped a few areas as if he had done this many times before, and there was a slight, glowing pulse from the device buried in her neck. Instantly, painlessly and without warning her mind went blank. She would have no recollection of these events. She would be transported to a local hospital where she would be placed overnight in a ward. Hospital staff would look confused by her arrival until the man accompanying her showed them some identification. Their acceptance of his obvious authority would be instant, there would be no questions, no arguments, just a complete and thorough execution of his instructions.

Once placed in the bed, the device in her neck would pulse gently, unnoticed by the hospital staff. As suddenly as her memories disappeared, they would return again, only they would not be complete, now they would be made up only of selective recollections. Virtually everything would remain intact – she would recall everything about her life, her childhood, her family – everything would still be there. Only details of the arrangement with the doctor and his organization had been suppressed. They were not needed right now. They might be recalled later, but for now all that she would know is that she had woken up in a hospital after fainting while giving blood.

Her husband would be on his way. For the man who accompanied her to the hospital, this was over for now. Without speaking to the woman or the hospital staff, he left the building. He had been in this hospital before, with this woman, three years before. Nobody even noticed him driving off in the black car.

Tranquility

Earth looked so calm from space, but within the darkness, there was inevitable devastation. This was unavoidable.

Planes started to drop from the skies, their pilots so surprised that they barely had time to register what was going on before they were overcome by the blackness.

Vehicles hurtled off roads, trains failed to stop when they reached their destinations and ships sailed on aimlessly at sea. All over the planet there was death, destruction, carnage.

It had to be this way. Thousands, maybe even millions of lives were lost that day.

Conditions were set up as well as they could have been to avoid as much of this as was possible.

There was really only one thing that could have made this the preferable option. And that was preventing the annihilation of all human life.

On Screen

He was thinking about Trudie again. Unseen by him, there was a faint, pulsing glow from a device that had been placed in his neck. As if recalling a memory that was locked deep down in his mind, he suddenly knew what to do. He had received instructions from another place. He had been trained for this, this equipment, this entire workstation was familiar to him.

He was not aware of what had just happened – it was not painful, there was no sensation at all. It was just the seamless fusion of thoughts that were not his own with his own consciousness. He couldn't even tell that it was happening. He knew however that he must activate his screen and check the outside perimeter of the bunker. This was simply a routine activity, at this stage of the operation all life on the surface would have been placed into stasis. He didn't question or challenge this, he just knew it to be so. He now had to perform this routine security operation. Standard military procedures. Secure the perimeter. He didn't expect there to be anything on the screen, of course. After all, how could there be?

The only life on the planet was in this bunker. This was the base from which the entire operation was to be managed.

It was impossible to avoid the effects of the darkness, all life had been subsumed by its force. So why was it that there were two human life forms showing up on the screen and they were just outside the main blast doors?

Chapter Six

New Home

I'm not sure if the food really is amazing or whether I'm just so ready to eat that I would gobble up anything at this moment. I'm just as ready to devour the information that Kate is about to give me. I decide to eat and listen.

Sometimes, there's just so much that you want to know that the only way to satisfy your thirst for the knowledge is to dump that information directly into your brain. That's not possible just yet – though I'm sure somebody in Silicon Valley will figure it out one day! So I let Kate talk, enjoy my food, and resist the urge to interrupt and take her off at a tangent. And let me assure you, that's a real breakthrough for me.

'I know you're desperate to know what's going on, Dan,' begins Kate, 'and the best thing I can do is to work down the list in order of priorities and try to reassure you as much as possible.'

She's good at this. She takes control, but not in a bossy way. She's kind and reassuring, and that's exactly what I need.

I remember Dad talking in similar terms about somebody in HR who he was dealing with when he left his job. Only his description ended with the words 'Except he turned out to be a viper!' Still, at this moment in time, Kate is the best chance I have of moving forward. I'll reserve judgement on the 'viper' bit.

'The first thing I need to let you know is that your dad, brother and sister are absolutely fine,' she continues. 'Nobody was hurt when the sirens went off, they were with us all the time in complete safety.' I breathe an internal sigh of relief. Three down, Mum to go, and then we're all accounted for.

'I know you must be really worried about your mum, Dan,' she says with a concerned look on her face. 'We didn't know there was another member of your family, and at this moment in time, I'm very sorry, but we do not have enough information to be able to tell you what happened to her.'

The feeling of hope that I'd had moments earlier suddenly subsides.

'In fact, we were really fortunate to have found you, Dan, you're a very lucky young man,' she goes on. 'It's a good job your dad was able to let us know your exact whereabouts after the lights came on.'

Somehow, I'm not feeling very lucky. Lucky is when a visiting relative draws a tenner out of their pocket and gives it to you as a gift, no strings attached. Lucky is finding that your brother and sister – and mum and dad come to that – have managed to leave that last chocolate biscuit in the fridge for you. Lucky is not getting to spend twenty-four hours alone in complete darkness in the entrance of a Cold War bunker. And having to pee in the corner too. Thank goodness it was dark at the time, I hope they didn't have night vision on the security cameras. Lucky is not having to watch your mum disappear as sirens wail for some crisis outside and the only doors that might offer her sanctuary are going to close tight before she can reach them. I keep my thoughts to myself, but I certainly don't feel very lucky at the moment.

'Now, I'm sure you'll want to know what's going on, Dan?' Kate asks.

I nod and attempt an answer with a mouth full of burger. Not a good move. Kate notices the mess I'm making and thankfully carries on.

'Dan, I have to tell you that you and your family got caught up in something very high-level. This is not even a national situation; I can confirm that this is an international operation.'

I swallow the lump of burger, but having heard what I've just heard, it is not an easy swallow to make.

'Dan, all of the people working in this bunker were specially trained and recruited for this mission – but even we do not know exactly what is going on yet.'

This is not sounding very reassuring.

'We know three things,' she continues. 'Firstly, the situation beyond the bunker is not life threatening to the people outside.'

More relief. I can tell already that my emotions are going to get a real workout in this place. At least this sounds like positive news for Mum.

'Secondly, as I said earlier, we have all been specially selected and recruited for this mission, but we have been trained individually to maintain the integrity and the security of the task. We do not yet know what's going on and we will not receive a full briefing for another eight hours.'

Okay, so far so good, she still hasn't mentioned 'imminent peril' or 'global annihilation'.

'Thirdly and finally, Dan,' she says, as I notice that the technique of using my name a lot in sentences has a strangely reassuring effect on me, 'you and your family were not supposed to be here when the sirens went off, only essential personnel had been tasked to be present at the time the sirens sounded. Even we didn't know that everybody else in the bunker at that time was going to be part of the mission team.

'Here's the strange thing that we're trying to figure out though,' she says, sounding much more serious now. 'We checked your biometrics when you were in the MedLab, and although your family aren't supposed to be here, you have full access rights on the database. In short, you were meant to be here.'

Within The Darkness

Although many, many lives had been lost, this was not the worst that it could have been. Just as many lives had been saved by the actions of governments throughout the world. It was not usual for the global community to work together in this way. But the consequences of not doing so would have been unthinkable.

Even places like North Korea, where the leaders and politics are caricatured every day in the western press, and ostracized from the international community, even they were complicit in this. Yes, this global action had already saved thousands of lives, possibly even millions. And most importantly, it would save more lives. Not only now, but in generations to come.

Every military leader understands the term 'collateral damage'. Deaths, injuries, destruction … lives lost, lives ruined. It is all acceptable, so long as the final objective is attained. When that objective is the survival of humanity itself, any military leader would understand that 'collateral damage' is going to be pretty high.

Beyond The Doors

She was supposed to have been gone for just a few minutes. She had to be quick for Harriet's sake, she was still a bit clingy for her mum. But better to go alone, she didn't want a scene from Harriet as they passed the sweets and souvenirs in the ticket area. For goodness' sake, the car was only parked just beyond the innocent looking cottage where they'd entered the bunker from the surface about an hour earlier. Five minutes tops.

She'd promised the kids that they could have 'tech-time' in the bunker café. Thank goodness they had free Wi-Fi in the bunker. Imagine, a holiday cottage with no Wi-Fi, who even does that these days? She was supposed to be one of the 'responsible adults', but even she was getting grouchy without the constant broadband speeds that they all enjoyed at home. And to get a phone signal from the holiday cottage, you had to go upstairs on to the landing and stand by the window. Sometimes even she had to do a double-check to make sure that she hadn't been transported back to pre-Jacobite Scotland. She had to remember Dan's phone too, he'd specifically asked her.

At her age, and she was only in her late thirties, if she didn't write it down or keep chanting it to herself, she forgot it. 'Laptop, Harriet's juice and Dan's phone …' she kept saying to herself. 'Laptop, Harriet's juice and Dan's phone …' she repeated as she stepped out of the cottage door into the car park. The first thing that struck her was how overcast it had become. More than overcast, the sky looked thunderous. She'd never seen anything like this before, the weather had been pretty bad anyway in the last few days, but this was really something. Still, it must just be the Scottish weather. As fierce as the midges.

She made for the car, which wasn't too far away from the entrance, and fumbled for the keys in her pocket. As she looked up towards the car, ready to point the remote at the door, she thought she saw… she was positive, there was somebody in the car. About the same height as Dan, same age or thereabouts, she thought.

Had she had slightly more time she might have experienced a glimmer of recognition as she moved up closer to the car to investigate what was going on. But at that precise moment, where indignant anger had kicked in and she'd started to march towards this youngster like a bad-tempered bull, a blue light, almost imperceptible to the naked eye, had begun to glow beneath the skin of her neck, and that momentary spark of recognition was extinguished in the gathering darkness overhead.

Training

For a task of this size and importance, absolute security was a must. That's why those chosen had to pass over a hundred psychometric tests before they even became a contender. And they didn't even know they were doing these tests. We so casually accept the role of the web and the internet in everyday life. A social media ad here, a search engine promo there, a 'please tell us how we did' survey popping up out of nowhere; online lives could so easily be hijacked and nobody was any the wiser. Most people got excited about data sharing and privacy issues. If they only knew what his organization was doing – with full global consent – the occasional highly targeted advert from an online retailer would be the least of their worries.

So it was that he'd managed to invisibly deliver thousands of psychometric evaluations and thus target his specialist team. These people had to be very carefully chosen. They weren't the strongest, the fastest, the cleverest or the wisest. All of the things that society generally applauded or celebrated had no currency when assembling this team. And there certainly weren't any celebrities in there either. Test after test had shown that the most remarkable people were often the most ordinary people. Sports stars excel at sport, film stars excel at acting, professors excel at being clever and heroes excel at heroism. But in the grave matter of saving the whole of humanity, it was a very carefully selected group of ordinary people who were going to make the final cut.

Two Figures

If it weren't for the pulsing device buried beneath the skin on his neck, he'd normally have been inquisitive about these two life forms just outside the blast doors. But instead, he calmly ran through a series of routines, just as he was taught to do in training. He was not an automaton in this task. While he was carrying it out, he still thought about Trudie and the kids.

He was aware of his surroundings and he heard in the background the 'getting to know you' conversations of a team who were just getting used to their new environment. They didn't know what their mission was yet, but their workstations were familiar, just as they were in their training and orientation. It was almost as if certain memories, feelings, or emotions, were being suppressed with a deft puppeteer pulling his strings so subtly that you'd barely be aware that it was actually a toy before your eyes. So he just watched the life forms on his screen and switched to camera surveillance. Just blackness. Night-vision mode. Still blackness. Penetration mode.

There they were! Two figures.

If he'd looked a little closer, if the camera had given a little more definition in that terrible, dark blackness – and particularly if that implant hadn't been pulsing away madly – he might have realized that he already knew that woman whose face was currently taking up half of his screen.

Chapter Seven

News

I'm stunned by what Kate has just told me. I'm a kid, how can I have a guest pass to this place?

'What about the others?' I ask. 'Dad, Harriet and David, did they pass the biometrics thingy?'

Okay, I know that isn't the most eloquent way to express myself, but I'm dealing with a lot of new information here.

'Unfortunately not,' replies Kate.

There are just two words in that short sentence, and I get an uneasy feeling that there might be a bit more information concealed behind that brief reply .

'Where is Dad?' I ask. I can hardly believe myself, such an obvious question, but if they are safe, why haven't I been reunited with my family yet?

'Well, that's where I do have a slightly less positive update for you, Dan,' Kate replies.

I can see that she is gearing up to something. She's figuring out the best words to use to deliver bad news.

'Your dad, brother and sister are not on the biometrics database. We can't explain that. So they do not have authorization to be here.'

Did I say 'bad news?' I mean, terrible news.

'Strictly speaking, Dan, they were supposed to be outside when the sirens sounded. They got trapped in here when the bunker doors closed; they're really not meant to be in the bunker.'

This is getting worse. I have a feeling that so far, from her point of view, this is the easy bit that she is delivering.

'Dan, your family have to stay contained during active operations as they do not have clearance to be here. You are not subject to those same restrictions, but we can't explain yet why you're classed as 'mission critical', it may well be an error.

'In the meantime, although you have the freedom of the bunker, you are not yet permitted under bunker protocols to see the other members of your family.'

A Simple Mission

He knew that what he did was top secret work, he understood that. He knew that he couldn't ask any questions and that orders had to be followed without question. That's how these things work. If you can't live with that, get a job at the local council offices. But this mission had troubled him. He was only supposed to have driven past those kids to get a really close video image of them. For face mapping or something similar, he wasn't involved in what happened after the initial job was done.

It was simple enough, for goodness' sake. The black car that came with the job was military grade. It looked like a regular car, could even generate a random number plate to keep it off police records if need be. If you wanted to, you could even show no number plate if you needed to be completely anonymous, and this thing was amazing to drive. In fact, it drove itself if you had to take your hands off the wheel. A feature often required in really delicate operations. Like this one.

Three dimensional, biometrics imaging. Whatever that means. He was a 'hired hand' not a scientist. He just gathered the data. And kept his mouth shut. And they gave him some great kit to do his job.

So why had the car swerved itself at the last minute, killing that kid?

The Sirens

She approached the person sitting in the car, the faint, blue pulsing light beneath her skin flickering furiously. Whatever its function, it was working overtime. Suppressing something very strong – an emotion, a thought, a connection. As she went to open the car door, a siren started to sound. She dismissed it at first, thinking it was part of the 'tourist experience' at the bunker.

It's odd, even though that siren wail has been used since the Second World War, then adapted for the Cold War, there is still nothing that can get anywhere close to it when it comes to the sound of grim portent. You couldn't replace it with a digital version, for instance – there's nothing that could assume anywhere near to its gravity and sense of impending crisis.

So when the siren continued to sound, the woman knew intuitively that something was up. It may have been prompted by that implant, but it fused her real thoughts, feelings and actions so seamlessly with those devised by her invisible puppeteer, that no observer would have been able to tell which part came from her real self and which part was artificially created.

'Come with me!' she demanded of the figure in the car, holding out her hand in a manner that showed that this was not up for discussion. It didn't matter what this person was doing in her car, why they had her laptop open and how they even got in there in the first place. She knew with all the certainty that she'd ever had in her life that taking shelter in the bunker was the best – the only – thing to do.

The device was able to suppress and hide her most powerful maternal emotions, yet seemed to miss the thing that landed them in so much jeopardy. 'Dan's phone!' she exclaimed, halfway across the car park.

Ridiculous that she would risk losing time to retrieve a mobile phone. Like the animal owner who leaps into the river to save their dog, only to perish while the dog swims happily to the river bank. Crazy actions at crazy times.

If it wasn't for the seconds that she'd lost retrieving Dan's phone, they'd have made it to the blast doors. If it wasn't for those lost, precious moments, she might have had time to glance to her right where a distinctive, black car was parked. Unusually, it had no number plate.

Chapter Eight

Uncertainty

I can't say that I really understand the meaning of the word 'protocols' but I certainly get the sense of Kate's last sentence.

'You mean I can't see them at all?' I query. Kate's eyes narrow. 'The viper?' I wonder to myself.

'Dan, I'm sorry, but until we receive a full mission definition, we have to observe the protocols.'

That word again. And she's using my name in each of her sentences. That's wearing a bit thin now. I can hear the words coming out of your mouth, I can hear you trying to get some rapport going here, but what you're telling me is not making me happy.

'What's mission definition?' I think to myself. I'm learning a lot today. I didn't hear the words 'mission definition' very often when Dad and I were laughing at online videos of cats as part of my home education. In fact, there wasn't much 'mission definition' in my life at all until I started talking to Kate. I decide to focus on what's important.

'So, where does that leave me?' I ask.

'You have the freedom of the bunker, and you may access all Green Zone areas,' she replies, 'But Red Zone areas are out of bounds to you.'

Funny how you can find yourself in the most hi-tech place you've ever been, yet you can't beat the colours red and green to tell you what you can – and can't – do.

'I also need to give you a tour of the bunker. I'm guessing it looks pretty different since you last saw it?'

'A bit of an understatement that, Kate.' She's got me at it now, I'm using her name in my sentences. It helps to build rapport, you know.

'What about Mum?' I ask again. I'm not sure what I mean about Mum, I just want some sort of action plan. Some 'mission definition'.

'As part of standard, start-up schemata, we sweep

the perimeters to check for life forms outside the bunker gates,' Kate answers. 'That process will be underway as I speak to you now. It's a basic security measure, but in this case we'll be looking for your mum.'

Schemata. Another new word to add to my vocabulary.

'If I hear anything, I'll let you know straight away.'

Quiet

Had he recognized that face on the screen, he might have moved with more urgency. He certainly would have been very surprised to see that particular person on the screen in front of him. They were connected. It was some years ago and at the time it was very significant to both of them.

For the person who'd engineered this reunion, it couldn't have had any more significance. It was as if a puppeteer was working through the script in a performance, each step carefully devised and planned to make sure it moved carefully towards the crescendo, the plotted course, the final outcome. It was no random thing that they happened to be in this place at this time. But when they'd first met, neither of them had a family, it had genuinely been a chance meeting back then. He now had Trudie and the kids. She had Mike, David, Harriet, Dan and Nat ... not Nat. Nat had died. But it was almost a lifetime ago for both of them. So much was different since then. So much water under the bridge, so many changes.

An apparent arbitrary meeting that had been working up to this reunion all these years later. What could have made this event so crucial right now? It made no difference to either of them at this moment. He was unable to recognize her because of the device implanted in his neck. She was unaware in the terrible darkness beyond the bunker blast gates that she and her young companion were even being watched.

Yet what was it that linked these two people so inextricably that it should be crucial to the world beyond the bunker that they met once again at this place, inside this underground shelter? If they had met each other again under normal circumstances, they would have worked it out straight away. It was those terrible events that they got caught up in while they were both serving in the Army.

Global

Ordinary people for an extraordinary job. The future of humanity no less. The problem with the 'high achievers' is that they tend to be too good. Brilliant – at only one thing. They spend hours, days, months and years honing their skills, ridiculous amounts of time mastering every element of their profession and then they become masters. But in becoming exemplary at one thing, they lose their focus and skills in many other areas. And ordinary people were exactly what he needed right now, for this particular mission.

Sure, these recruits had to be fit, bright, sharp and intelligent. But they also needed to be average. Not just any kind of average though. They had to be the very best at being average. Being average means that you can do many things to an average standard. One minute you can be fit, the next you can be strategic. You can pivot from that to being an average problem solver, an average technical operator or an average fighter. Yes, in this scenario being average at many things was exactly what he required.

This mission had never been attempted before and even he could not anticipate what skills, challenges and problems lay ahead. So in this scenario, average was about as good as it was going to get.

Sadness

He was used to being impartial about his work. He knew it had to be done, most of the time it was just surveillance or moving people from one place to another. But this was something else. He had not been responsible for the car swerving. His hands were off the wheel, the car took over the minute that was detected by the sensors. The car's internal computer knew to adjust speed, maintain distance from the kerb, scan for all life forms and 'anticipate' other vehicles. It could 'recognize' double yellow lines, 'Stop' signs, 'Give Way' road markings and even a school crossing attendant. And this was a military-grade vehicle.

While commercial organizations made a big deal about driverless cars and how they were 'the future', they were wasting their time; the military had been on to this concept for many years. If it works with drones, it works with cars. 'Military' might not be the right word to use though. It was definitely 'military-like', it felt governmental and it was certainly top-secret. But he wasn't quite sure who he worked for. And that didn't matter to him before he – before his car – hit that child. But it's all he'd thought about since then. He was no killer.

He had no instructions to kill on that day. He'd been unable to stop it, just forced to look into the eyes of one of the children and watch it happen. The only way it could have occurred is because of computer error. Unlikely. He hesitated to say 'impossible', but it really was pretty well impossible. As impossible as anything could be. No, he was sure it had something to do with the man who'd distracted the mother as he'd just driven by. The face that he recognized straight away, in spite of the disguise and even though he was completely out of place. He should not have been at that place at that time. It was his boss, Doctor Pierce.

Chapter Nine

Last Moments

She rushed past the black car, failing not only to notice its familiarity but also the very obvious fact that something was not quite right. It had no registration plate. Had this been anything other than a desperate race to get back to her family, she might have glanced back.

Something out of place might have registered with her. Had she looked back, she would have seen that number plate change before her eyes. From being totally blank, to generating a random registration number. Something that the police would never be able to trace. Had she noticed what was going on, she might have wondered 'What kind of car can do that?'

And if the device in her neck wasn't doing its job quite so well, she might have realized that she'd been travelling in that very car only a few days earlier.

Tour

It seems on the surface that I'm talking to the most pleasant person on the Earth. She even uses my name regularly in her sentences. To build rapport. So why do I get an uneasy feeling whenever Kate speaks to me?

She appears to be helping me, giving me the information that I am asking for. I want this, I need to know these answers and this information. So why does it all seem to be bad news? Everything she says seems to be a block – a 'No' – yet the way that she says it sounds as if it is a positive thing.

I know what Dad meant about that guy in HR now. 'A viper'. He must have felt the same thing when he left his job. I don't feel that I am much further forward. What do I know? Mum is missing, but is probably okay. That's about it.

They are looking for her. I can't progress that, I'm in their hands on that one. Dad, Harriet and David are safe. I haven't seen them with my own eyes, and even though I am unsure of Kate, I do believe her that they are okay at least. They might have been in the wrong place at the wrong time. The worst that could happen would be that they were restricted to a certain area. The Red Zone probably.

And what about me? How did I get lucky? And why am I on the 'biometrics database' or whatever she called it? I know I've joined a lot of random mailing lists but I'm pretty sure that there's nothing too sinister about most of the gaming sites that I visit. I'm certain I didn't get myself onto any biometrics database. I really must read the terms and conditions more carefully next time I register.

I decide to focus on the facts. Dad, Harriet and David are alive and fine. Mum is alive – and I hope she's fine. I'm certainly feeling much better after my time in the MedLab – or whatever it was that Kate called it – and the burger and chips that I just ate seem to have enabled amazing recuperative powers.

'Am I okay to take a look around?' I ask Kate, 'Get a feel for the place?'

'No problem!' Kate replies, pleased to get away from the tricky and troublesome topics, I suspect. She looks very relieved that I'm changing the subject.

'Kate,' I ask, remembering that there's one more thing that I want to ask her right now, 'how did this place change so much, from the old bunker that we saw? It seems incredible, it's like it's a different place.'

Happy to move on to other matters, Kate introduces me to yet another new word. Who needs home ed when you get to spend the day in a hi-tech, space-age military-style bunker? It's doing wonders for my vocabulary.

'Transmogrification,' Kate declares.

This has the sound of something unpleasant that might happen to a cat.

'Transformation using nanotechnology,' Kate continues. 'A technological based process that completely changes the interior of the building. It's not technology that I've ever seen before, I think I'm probably as amazed as you are.'

'How does it happen while we're right in the middle of it?' I wonder aloud.

'When the sirens sounded, everybody inside the bunker went to the Holding Area. The bunker staff recruited for this mission had been briefed to do that, and our first role was to move any civilians who were in the vicinity into the Holding Area with us – pending formal clearance to leave and assume our duties.

'We got to your dad and brother and sister just in time to secure them with us in the Holding Area.

'The change process happened while the lights were out ...'

She pauses as if considering whether to tell me something.

'We're still not quite sure why there was such a long delay with the lights coming back on.'

'How come I got away with it, as I wasn't inside the safe room with you?' I ask, genuinely intrigued by this conversation now.

'You got lucky,' Kate replies. 'The entrance is only a superficial transformation; if furniture, fixtures and fittings are involved I'm guessing it gets a bit messy!'

Whatever this was, it was pretty incredible. This place has been completely transformed. I know it's the same building, the shape and layout is the same, but it's as if the team from that home makeover show on TV have been let loose on the place after drinking way too much coffee.

'How come you came to get me in those anti-virus suits too?' I ask, squeezing out one last question.

'We hadn't had time to ascertain if the corridor was 100 percent free of any external contamination at that time, so protocols state that until we've completed that process, we have to use the suits ... sorry if we frightened you!' she adds in, remembering that she is talking to a youngster rather than an adult.

I ask Kate if it's okay if I take a look around on my own. For someone who just spent twenty-four hours alone in the dark, I'm feeling quite plucky now.

Burgers and sleep are amazing things, they can completely restore me.

'Fine,' she says, 'you're on surveillance wherever you go and your biometrics will only give you access where you have clearance.'

I'm not sure if this is useful information or a warning. As in 'Don't go anywhere you're not supposed to.'

'No problem,' I say and I'm on my way, fuelled by a space-age burger.

I can remember most of the layout from my previous walk through, and even though it's completely different in appearance, I can still find my way around as the corridor layout is exactly the same. Red Zone rooms are visibly marked as are Green Zone rooms. Even I can follow that. To get through any door you place your hand on a pad. Presumably it scans your hand in some way – something to do with your biometrics whatever it was – as I'm never blocked wherever I go.

The dormitories – Green Zone – no problem. The chapel – Green Zone – no problem. The broadcasting studio – Green Zone – no problem. Only it's not a broadcasting studio any more. Now it's a gym. I won't be needing that right now – or anytime soon – so I make my exit swiftly.

As I walk through to the doors, I notice an area just along the corridor that I haven't spotted before: Red Zone. Look, I'm sixteen years old, what do you expect? It was only a matter of time until I tried one of the hand pads on a Red Zone door. I know I'm on camera, I don't try to hide it, because I expect to be denied access. No big deal.

When I put my hand on the pad, I'm half

expecting that 'Uh-uh' sound that they use on that family quiz show when somebody messes up an answer. Maybe Mum's right, too much time spent watching old clips on video websites. So there's nobody more surprised than me when I place my hand on the pad and the door opens.

It's dark inside at first, but the lights are wired to come on as soon as someone enters. It takes my eyes a short time to adjust, but as they do, they fall on three figures in what I can only describe as 'pods'. They're wired up to all sorts of electronic gadgetry, and they're unaware of me.

At first, I think I've stumbled on some kind of sleeping area, but I saw the dormitories only a few minutes ago. They were Green Zone. This is Red Zone.

These three figures are not sleeping. They're unconscious, restrained, they're being kept that way by the gadgetry.

I recognize one of them: she was the lady who gave us our tickets when we came in – these must be the staff. Used to serving tourists. Caught up in something by accident. 'Unauthorized personnel' is what Kate would probably call them. Or 'Unauthorized personnel, Dan' more likely. Building more rapport.

One of the lights in the room flickers into life as I move further into the room. I don't know why – or how – I got into this room, but I'm very pleased I did.

As the light adjusts to full brightness and my eyes acclimatize, I focus on another three figures held captive in these sinister pods. It's Dad, David and Harriet.

Chapter Ten

Blast Doors

The device that quietly and undetectably pulsated in her neck was made of extremely advanced technology. Only a very limited number of people knew its source. It worked very cleverly in the background; she was completely unaware of its effect upon her consciousness. Those who knew how to look for the devices would have immediately spotted that it was currently in 'receive' mode. Somebody was controlling her thoughts, but not in a robotic way. Her device emitted a faint blue light. The untrained eye might have mistaken it for a vein in her neck. The trained eye would have looked specifically at the colour, because that was the most crucial thing. Blue, red, yellow, purple, black or green – it made all the difference. She had full consciousness and complete knowledge of what was going on around her.

She was not aware that her recognition of the child in the car had been suppressed by the device, but it had been, working away undetected in the background, filtering out the elements that would create a strong emotional response. Things that might distract her right now. It was very subtle. So as she rushed past the black car with her new companion, there was no glimmer of recognition. Neither the child nor the car registered in her memory, even though she was aware of both. She knew that there were questions to be asked about why the child had been in the car in the first place, but it was as if her attention had been caught by something else.

She had a very strong and compelling sense that

she must take shelter in the bunker. But she'd come for the laptop, juice and Dan's phone, and she'd even returned to the car to get one of them. She knew too that there was urgency and that they would have to hurry.

The sky was now darkening quickly; this appeared to be much more than a storm. It was unworldly. She knew it must be freak weather conditions, maybe a solar effect or something similar, but she instinctively felt that the siren and the darkness were linked.

The two figures rushed towards the cottage, through the doors, and with massive urgency they tried to make up for those few lost seconds when she'd returned to the car. They approached the bunker doors just too late. If only they hadn't returned for the tech. They would have made it if they'd not wasted those vital moments. They approached the run-up to the blast doors as the gap between them began to narrow to a close. There was just time to see Dan's face and hear his calls to them as the heavy doors shut tightly with a deep and final rumble. They were all alone.

Deceit

I'm stunned for a few moments as I look at the still forms of three members of my family in their glass pods. They are unharmed; I can see that no physical damage has been done to them. I can also figure out enough from the screens and dials surrounding them to see that they are alive.

I'm not totally sure what I'm looking at, but I've seen enough hospital dramas to know that these are monitoring life signs, and Dad, David and Harriet all have constantly pulsing heart rates and lively brain activity. In fact, David's brain activity looks really lively on the screen. He must be thinking about his online game sites again. My instinct is not to panic, but I am suddenly pretty angry.

It's okay Kate saying that they have to 'stay contained' because they don't have clearance. I can accept that. After all, the alternative is to be trapped beyond the bunker doors. I'm happy that they're okay. But I assumed that being 'contained' would mean being held in a comfortable room somewhere together. I didn't think it would mean being frozen or put to sleep … or whatever it is that has been done to them.

The other thing that's bothering me is that Kate has deceived me. She hasn't actually told me any lies, but she hasn't told me the whole truth either. For instance, my family are being held in a Red Zone area. I'm only supposed to have Green Zone access, so I'm not supposed to be seeing this. It makes me wonder what else is going on in the other Red Zone rooms.

And even more intriguing is why I can get access to these areas. It has to be some terrible computer error or glitch. Maybe they use the same dodgy operating system that I'm stuck with on my laptop.

At the moment, I need to stay focused. I'm the best hope for Dad, David and Harriet. If I end up in one of these pods too, we'll be at the mercy of whoever is running this place. I don't get the feeling that anything sinister is going on, but I'd still rather be conscious and moving than stuck in one of these glass coffins.

'Don't call them coffins,' I think. But that's what they remind me of. Bearing in mind what's happened in the past day or two, I'm pretty impressed with how maturely I figure out what needs to come next. Dad would be proud of me – if he was awake. I need to be cool about this situation, because if I cause trouble, I'll probably end up in the same place as all the other 'civilians' in this room.

If I end up here, I won't be able to figure out what's going on. Dad needs me to make sure that somebody is looking out for them. And there's Mum too. I can't bear ending up in here and not knowing what's happened to her. So everybody needs me to play the game with Kate and just keep things ticking over. For some reason I've got clearance to roam freely. Who knows why? That might change when they have more time to acclimatize to their new surroundings, or when they get their mission instructions. The best bet is to stay cool, keep off the radar and maintain a low profile. Great strategy, Dan. Because at that very moment, Kate bursts into the room with two armed guards at her side.

The World Sleeps

The darkness crept across the surface of the Earth, obliterating all light, filling all spaces that it encountered. It began with the skies, but it moved across the Earth, permeating the seas, blocking the sun's rays, extinguishing all flames.

Many things could be planned for in advance. Nuclear power stations closed down, one by one, under government instructions. Just a routine drill, a test for a 'national emergency'. It didn't matter what the excuse was, they were used to instructions like this 'from above'. They just did what they were told, when they were told.

Most flights were grounded, but you can't account for everything. In matters like these, you can't save everybody. What else can you do if you need the whole world put to sleep for a while? Some lives are bound to be lost.

All in all, it was as well executed as you could hope for. So that when the freak global weather patterns turned from grey skies, to black, and then something much, much more sinister, most of the world had pretty well stopped itself.

When the final surge of blackness came, there was just enough time for the internet to go crazy with conspiracy theories, religious predictions and apocalyptic scenarios.

If only they had known before they slipped into that deep slumber, the biological stasis that the darkness brought with it. This was no Doomsday scenario. The darkness had been unleashed across the planet specifically to prevent the destruction of the Earth.

Conscience

Loyalty can be a funny thing. It can change in the blink of an eye. He'd never before questioned the work that he was doing or the tasks that he was asked to do. He understood that governments have to act for the 'common good' and that sometimes people had to do things that might make the 'ordinary' man or woman uncomfortable. But being responsible for the death of a child? That can never be justified. So on the day that he drove away from that desperate scene, his loyalties changed. As the sight of a crowd gathering around a dying child at the roadside grew smaller in his rear-view mirror, his conscience kicked in. He knew that he could not question his orders or challenge what had just happened.

He couldn't even explain it. Asking questions, making waves and prying into the mission outcomes would not get him any closer to the truth. He would need to maintain his cover, keep his poker face on. But he was not a child killer. And he was not going to let the loss of a child's life go unchallenged.

Nor was he a fool. The machinations of the shadowy figures in his organization sometimes took years to play out. So it would be with the death of this child. He was a patient man; he knew the importance of the long game. So he would wait and watch. But the death of this child had not gone unnoticed. And he would make sure that the young life that he had just helped to end would not go unavenged.

Chapter Eleven

Grounded

Kate looks as much troubled as she does annoyed. She can't explain how I got in here, but she knows that she's going to have to think of something quickly. And I must have the same look on my face that I did when Mum caught me hunting in her wardrobe for my birthday presents. That guilty look of somebody who knows that they've just been caught red-handed and knowing that they have some serious explaining to do.

Fortunately, Kate speaks first.

'Dan, we're really disappointed to find you in

here,' she begins.

Darn, she used the 'disappointed' word. I remember everybody wheeling out that one when I was having my problems at school.

'The incredible thing is that you seem to have full clearance across the bunker,' she continues, 'so you are in fact authorized to be here.'

Phew, advantage Dan. She doesn't want me here, she doesn't like me being here, but it appears that there's not much that she can do about it.

Time to go on the offensive, but she gets in before me.

'We need to explain what's going on, Dan. I'm sure you must be shocked to find your family like this?' she says.

Kate is good. In fact she's very good. She has this knack of seeing what's going on in my head, then dealing with it in a way that answers all of my questions. Yet it leaves the biggest questions unanswered still.

How does she manage that? I think back to Dad and his rants about the HR people at his work. 'People must make a living out of this,' I think to myself, 'of saying one thing, then meaning another thing entirely.' Maybe politics will eventually make sense to me after all.

'Your Dad and your brother and sister are in stasis,' Kate explains.

I decide to let her say what she wants to say, uninterrupted. I hope Dad can't hear this, I wouldn't want him to think that this 'not interrupting' thing is going to become a habit anytime soon.

'They were exposed to the darkness beyond the blast doors when the sirens went off. You were all caught in the corridor.'

'So was I!' I interject.

'Here's the strange thing, Dan,' Kate continues.

She's doing that 'Dan' thing again. It works every time with me.

'We checked you out thoroughly in the MedLab and you're absolutely fine,' she explains, raising another mystery rather than solving any.

'Your family and the bunker staff from the cottage may have got caught by the darkness as they made their way into the bunker when the sirens went off. It's essential that they remain in the pods for BioFiltration, it's for their own health – and safety,' she adds at the end.

'Health and safety,' I think. 'Even at the end of the world we have to do a risk assessment!' I keep my thoughts to myself and ask, more intelligently I hope, 'What is BioFiltration?'

'Great question!' Kate replies.

She knows she has won this exchange by engaging my curiosity. Have you ever noticed how brilliant you feel when someone says 'Great question?' It happened to me at school quite a lot. I'd put my hand up, ask something pretty obvious, like I was paying full attention. And the teacher would enthusiastically reply with a 'Great question!'

Now, don't get me wrong, I knew it really wasn't a great question. It was a diversionary technique I'd mastered many years ago. Be proactive with questions that you control, that way the teacher will see that you've participated in class. And when it comes to them asking questions over which you have no control, they'll pass you by. After all, you've already contributed. Diligent student that you are. But the

'Great question!' reply always works on me. It always makes me feel as if I've just done something amazing. When I know I haven't.

So while I'm patting myself on my own back for my great 'What is BioFiltration?' question, Kate gives me the answer.

'We don't have full information yet about what's happening outside the bunker, as you know, Dan, but we do know from the medical teams that the darkness itself is not harmful.'

Okay, so far so good, once again. She's very skilled at this reassurance lark.

'However, all of the people in this room were partially exposed to the darkness, when they're supposed to be either fully exposed, as with the people outside the bunker, or not exposed at all, as is the case with those of us who were inside all of the time. These BioFilters are removing the contaminated elements and restoring all vital signs to normal levels.'

Wow, I actually understand all of that. Maybe I am cut out to be a futuristic bunker worker after all.

'So in summary, Dan, your family are fine; all of the people in this room are fine. They just need to stay here for a little while longer while the process is completed. After that, we'll wake them up and you'll all be able to chat.'

'Great news!' I think to myself, and to be completely honest, although everything that's going on here is completely unfamiliar to me, I'm still not unduly worried. What Kate tells me all adds up. What I hear and what I see makes sense, I've no reason to doubt it.

We've all been standing still while we've been having this conversation and at that moment the movement-sensitive lights turn themselves off again. It's only a moment until somebody moves and they're back on again. But for the few seconds that the lights are out, I catch a glimpse of something. I'm sure that I saw a faint light where Kate's neck was in the darkness. Unusual, because it appears to be pulsating.

I can't see it as clearly now the lights have come on, though I am pretty sure that I've just seen it in the darkness.

It's a pulsating, faint light just at the side of her neck and it's coloured red.

Solo Mission

He stood up at his terminal and walked towards the exit. Nobody seemed to notice him. They saw him moving, but they were unable to detect the significance of what he was about to do. It was an unusual situation in the Control Room. They just seemed to be waiting.

They were waiting of course. The full mission briefing was coming in the next few hours. They knew that the assignment was connected to that. They knew that their loved ones beyond the doors would be fine. They'd had the advantage, they had been able to engineer things so that their families were at home when it began. Their initial instructions were simple. Just like they'd practised in training. Familiarize yourself with your workstation. Perform the routine tasks on your initial work schedule. Basic things such as 'Check the perimeter' and 'Ensure all terminals are operating correctly'. Then, use the time to familiarize yourself with the bunker layout and other team members. It was a simple holding pattern, prior to the full briefing taking place.

There was an atmosphere of hesitant expectation in the building, but assurances had been given, training had been thorough and all was as it was supposed to be. Except for James or 'Roachie' as his closest friends called him. He now had a personal mission which had to be completed secretly. This mission hadn't been communicated via his terminal or through any of the routes that were considered 'normal procedure'. James's actions were taken as a consequence of the device that was faintly pulsating beneath the skin on his neck. Barely perceptible unless you were looking for it. Its blue light seemed to suggest that information was being transmitted in some way. Unknown, invisible, undetected. James knew what he was doing, but he didn't understand the implications of the solo mission that he was about to carry out.

Had his consciousness been entirely under his own control, he would have known to alert his Control Room colleagues as to what he was about to do. He would have registered his whereabouts on the staff rota terminal as he left the Control Room. And he certainly would not have disabled the surveillance cameras and the alarm systems connected to the main bunker doors.

Impenetrable

If you could see through this blackness, you would have been able to view the lives of millions of human beings paused, as if somebody had just stopped time. The darkness was impenetrable. It was neither liquid nor gas, yet it crept across the surface of the Earth in a dense cloud and it sat in the atmosphere as if it were a heavy shroud.

If you ran your hand through the blackness you would feel nothing, neither would it be displaced, as it would have been if moving through smoke. It was dry to the touch, even though the atmosphere around it was not devoid of moisture.

Most striking of all was how dark it was. You could not see anything through it. It was all consuming, there were no gaps, no chinks of light, no areas untouched. And it just sat there, awaiting the moment when its purpose would become clear.

Army Life

She'd barely had a career in the Army before she was made redundant. It came fairly quickly after the incident. So while the HR people called it 'redundancy' she knew that there was really another reason why. Probably because she didn't do what she should have done. What else was she supposed to do?

She was a recent and very raw recruit, she'd had limited training and had received very little in the way of guidance from her superiors. She had just reacted on instinct. An ordinary, average person doing extraordinary things in a situation that they'd never encountered before. Most people would have been given a medal for what she did. But whatever it was that she'd done wrong, it must have caused a lot of trouble higher up. And look at the personal price she'd paid on that terrible day eighteen years ago. Not that it mattered of course, just look at her wonderful family now. Still, in spite of what happened and all of the fallout afterwards, at least there was one great result from that day. One thing that she'd never regretted, in spite of it all.

She'd saved a man's life that day. James was still alive because of her.

Chapter Twelve

On The Move

I'm not sure what the red light means, but now I've spotted it in the darkness, I'm finding it really hard to keep my eyes off it. With the lights on, knowing it's there, I can see just beneath the skin on Kate's neck. Interestingly, the two guards also have the same thing. I need to get to a mirror quickly. Do I have one of these things fitted? Is it part of whatever is going on in the bunker? Unusually for me, I decide to keep my mouth shut about it. Kate seems unaware of its presence, and like so many other things in this unfamiliar environment, it may just be something that all the staff have. I resolve to keep my eyes open to see if everybody here has one fitted.

I'm ready to excuse myself and head for the bathroom facilities along the main corridor so that I can check out my own neck. But Kate has other things in mind. She's explained what is going on here, but I've still been discovered in a Red Zone. Okay, I had clearance, but she'd explicitly asked me not to enter these areas.

'Dan, I need to make a very special request of you, is that okay?' she asks.

Interesting way of phrasing the question. Is 'No' really an option here?

'Yes, of course,' I reply. What a sucker.

'Although you have Red Zone authorization at the moment, I need to ask you to stay out of those areas for your own safety.'

I don't like the sound of those words: 'At the moment'. She sees this as an anomaly, a temporary thing.

'We're only a few hours away from receiving a full briefing, and what's going on beyond the bunker lies entirely in our hands. I'm sure an intelligent lad like you understands how important this is and that it's really crucial that we don't interfere with any mission critical issues before then.'

The 'intelligent lad' works just as well as the 'Good question' technique. I really must try to be less easily flattered.

'So what I'd appreciate is if you could restrict your access to Green Zone areas only until we receive the briefing? Is that a reasonable thing to ask, Dan?' she finishes.

Of course it's a reasonable thing to ask. But remember Kate, I'm a sixteen-year-old boy. I know what 'reasonable' is. I understand what 'reasonable' is. But I don't always like being 'reasonable'. However, I'm not going to pick any fights right now. I agree to restrict my movements to the Green Zones and keep out of the Red Zones until we get the full briefing. I reassure Kate that I don't want to put the lives of my family at risk. I tell her how important it is to me that we find my mum safe and make sure that she's properly looked after. And I hope she doesn't spot me using her own techniques on her. I'm a quick learner.

'I think that's a really great plan, Kate,' I smile.

Trapped

How could she have been so stupid as to go back for the tech? If she'd followed her instincts, they would have just had the time to get inside those doors before they closed. As it was, the darkness was swiftly closing in. Beyond the cottage it was beginning to look dark outside, even though it was mid-afternoon. Inside the cottage, even the lights were struggling; this was like no other darkness she'd ever seen before. She felt fine and her young companion seemed fine. She knew that she needed to seek shelter and the bunker seemed the best place to do it.

There didn't appear to be an immediate risk to them. What would she have told the kids to do? Wait by the entrance. It's the safest option. If anybody comes out of there, that's where they'll exit. If anybody goes in there, that's where they'll enter. In a situation where the choices were very limited, the best thing to do seemed to wait by the entrance. Unknown to her, Dan had made exactly the same decision on the other side of the doors.

So they waited, sitting down in fearful silence outside the huge red blast doors as they became surrounded by the darkness. It neither harmed them nor stopped them breathing, but its impenetrable blackness was completely debilitating. Any movement or conversation was completely out of the question.

She imagined that this must be similar to blindness, only her mind allowed her to picture the doors in front of them, the corridor behind them and her son only metres away, but all alone.

Waiting

He'd seen his chance when he was able to reconnect with the mother at the training centre. Driving her to the hospital and checking her in, it seemed as if she'd recovered okay after the accident. He didn't really converse with her, just did his job, but on the surface she looked to be fine.

It had been what the police called a 'cold case' since that horrible day when the car had hit the child. When he'd hit the child. He hadn't meant to, but he'd been the one in the car at the time. That sickening sound would live with him forever. Out of the blue, the mother of the dead child had ended up as a passenger in his car.

What were the chances of that? Very high as it turned out. He knew that in this line of work, things had a funny way of connecting. Often, completely unrelated people and events would come together.

It wasn't the actual car. But the same make. More gadgets, more tech, more devices than three years ago. But still the same car, same design, same black colour. Obviously the original had been destroyed. DNA – a great thing or a dangerous thing. All depends who you work for of course. He'd had time to plant a tracking device on her before he left her in the hospital. One that couldn't be traced by anybody else.

You didn't work in this line of business for so long without learning a few tricks. He'd actually bought it from a high street electrical store. Hilarious! They had all this kit, but never thought anybody capable of buying a few bits of electrical circuit from a local store. International espionage foiled by a tech junk.

Sure, he'd had to adapt it a bit. But you could fool the organization using bits of kit that anybody can buy for less than a tenner. He knew that if she had surfaced again, then the story was just about to become clearer.

Yes, you had to be very patient in this business. Random threads could appear from every direction and seem to have nothing at all in common. But he knew that the threads in this particular story were just being drawn together. He was sure that he'd discover the reason for the accident and how it all tied in together.

The tracker would help him to figure out why she had appeared back on the radar after three years away from it completely.

But when he realized where the tracker was taking him – following in his car a mile behind – he knew that this wasn't just going to be the conclusion of any old story.

This was where all the threads from his work were going to lead. This was the end game.

Chapter Thirteen

A Lucky Hunch

I'm amazed that Kate and the two security guys just let me go after that. I suppose that they'll know exactly where I'm going and what I'm up to from the surveillance cameras that are positioned wherever I go in this place. I assume that virtually every room I go into must be monitored too.

This place seems to run on biometrics and although I'm not entirely sure what that means, I suspect that everything I do here is directly tracked back to me. Which means that I can't really get away with anything. The best bet, as far as I can tell at present, is to carry on exploring and get a feel for this place. Really, we're all waiting for that mission announcement which must still be a few hours away. Plenty of time to have a good snoop around.

First though, I decide to head directly for the bathroom and shower areas because I want to get a look at my neck. I'm not really sure what happened to me in the MedLab earlier, I assume I was just checked over to make sure everything was fine.

That reminds me of another unusual thing that happened earlier. How come the darkness didn't have any impact on me? I was in the entrance area at the same time as Dad, David and Harriet, and the bunker staff from the cottage area were also coming below ground at that time. So why are they in the glass pods and I'm not? I'm feeling totally fine now. I'm almost embarrassed to admit that after the temporary discomfort of being all alone in that corridor for so many hours, and having stuffed myself with food, I'm back to 100 percent Dan. If they have put one of those weird, glowing things into my neck, I certainly can't detect it. Neither does it seem to be making any impact on me. I can't feel it pulsating or vibrating in any way, so I assume I don't have one. I enter the bathroom area and head straight for a mirror.

The light is unusual below ground, you can't quite catch the full light that you would if the area had a window. I inspect my neck closely, on both sides, but I can see and feel nothing. I'm reasonably sure I'm clear. I see a mirror that is lit better, so I go over to it and check again. Everything is fine. Whatever Kate and the security guys have going on, I seem to be well clear of it. I reckon it's probably just something bunker related. A communication device or something like that. But I resolve to check out everybody that I encounter from now on to see if they also have one of these devices fitted.

Satisfied that all is as it should be, I leave the bathroom area and start to walk along the corridor once again. It's very quiet here, the main hub at present must be in the Control Room, which I'm guessing has changed quite a lot since I last saw it. I'd expect that to be a Red Zone area and although, in theory, I'm allowed in there, I decide that the best strategy is to explore as many Green Zone areas as I can and just to take a mental note of anything unusual that is Red Zone.

There are two levels to the bunker; we explored them both thoroughly when I was here with the family. That was only a day ago, but so much has happened since then. I haven't really had time to think about what's going on outside. It's easy to forget down here, with no windows or view of the world beyond these thick walls. It's a strange sensation; it really does feel that outside doesn't exist anymore.

I'd really like to know what's being done about Mum. I was so distracted by trying to take care of my own interests in my last exchange with Kate that I didn't push that point.

It's good to know that she's okay, but I picture her locked outside the blast doors and hope that she's really alright. She'll probably end up in one of those pods before I get to see her, but at least if she winds up like Dad, David and Harriet, I'll know that she's safe. And who was that who was with her? I only caught a glimpse. Whoever it was, they were my sort of age and my sort of height. I'm doubting my judgement now. It can't have been Nat – that would be ridiculous. They certainly had the same look and hair colouring though.

So many questions, so few answers. There's nothing I can do to progress things right now, so I decide to head for Level 2. When we toured the bunker earlier, we bypassed the lift. It had looked pretty basic at that time but now, like everything else in this transformed bunker, it's definitely something that I want to try.

As I approach the lift, a member of the bunker staff gets in ahead of me.

'Just hold the doors please!' I shout, catching the lift before the doors close. I expect to see only two floor options in the lift, but there are four. Well, I say four, but there are also two unusually labelled buttons above the marker for Level 1. 'It must go up to the cottage,' I think to myself, 'but why two buttons?'

'Where do the other floors lead to?' I ask my companion in the lift.

'They're redundant,' she replies. 'There are only the two levels in this place, the rest are there in case they extend the bunker in future.'

She can see that I'm curious, so she presses buttons 3 and 4. Nothing happens. No lights, no noises, nothing at all.

'How about those two?' I ask, pointing at the unusual symbols above the button marked '1'. 'Nothing again,' she replies.

She presses both of them. Individually and then together. She must have kids in her life beyond the bunker; she's very patient. They must be young kids because she's very 'show and tell'.

'See,' she says. Again nothing. She presses the button for Level 2 and we begin our descent. I had been thinking that maybe it was just a simple case of a broken lift. But no, those buttons are not for use.

The lift arrives on Level 2, the doors open and the lady steps out, giving me a smile as she does so. I notice a faint, red pulsating light in her neck. It is very faint this time, I'd never have noticed it if I hadn't known to look carefully. 'Must just be something to do with all the people here,' I think to myself, resolving to ask Kate next time I see her.

I'm about to step out of the lift to begin my exploration of Level 2 when an attack of inquisitiveness makes me step back inside. I've never been one of those people who just accepts things at face value. Ask Mum; she'll tell you.

For instance, when she told me at age five not to touch the kettle because she'd just boiled it, what do you think I did? I opened the lid and touched the water with my finger of course! And when Mum asked me not to touch the kitchen blender when I was thirteen because the lid wasn't on, what do you think I did? Well I pressed the button of course! And created a massive mess of blended strawberries and bananas. So, after the kind lady tells me that the extra lift buttons don't work and even goes so far as to demonstrate – what do you think I do? I need to prove it to myself of course. Why would anybody add extra buttons if they weren't needed?

Everything has been designed very carefully in this place, I can't imagine anybody leaving a few spares around in case they'd forgotten anything. So, I decide to put it to the test. I press the weird symbols first. The first button, then the second button, then both of them together.

My heart gives a small jump. There is a glimmer of something when I touch the buttons together: a momentary jolt, but it stalls. One of the buttons is illuminated. I try again. Same again, a small jolt, but no movement. You have to press both buttons at once to get that though. One of the buttons remains illuminated.

'Okay, move on, Dan,' I think to myself. I press the third button.

When the woman had done it earlier, there was nothing. No sound, light or movement. But when I press the third button there is an instant response and the lift starts to move down to the next level.

Unseen

When the lady and the youngster re-entered the cottage, he'd immediately spotted the mother. He could guess what was happening outside, he'd prepared for it of course, but he didn't think that it was going to play out like this. In this place. And with these people involved. How did they link up with this? He didn't know yet, but he'd keep close because it was unlikely to end well. And after losing her child in that way, didn't she deserve to have someone like him looking out for her? Where did the kid come from? That might cause a problem later, but first things first.

The sirens were sounding; the first release must have begun. She was making her way to the bunker, the same as everybody else. That's where he needed to be too. He followed at a distance, an expert at not being seen, but was quick to realize that they were not going to make it to the bunker doors in time.

He knew that when the first release was completed they would not be able to see a thing. So, she was doing the best thing, the most sensible strategy was to wait by those doors. She was making good decisions under stress. Sooner or later they'd be spotted and he'd be able to get in. He'd just pretend to be bunker staff, nobody would know. He could patch in clearance levels when he got inside; should be simple enough.

So, as the woman and the child sat closely together on the left-hand side of the bunker doors, they were unaware that only a few feet away from them, standing in total silence and completely unknown to them, was the man who would be forced to shoot one of them in the next thirty-six hours.

Beyond The Blast Doors

There were two people beyond the blast doors. That's what the monitor indicated. It identified them both as human. It would not make any sense to open the doors to the bunker cat in a situation like this, so it was important to know who – or what – was out there.

One female – age thirty-seven and one male – age forty-eight. The female was sitting with an arm positioned as if she had it wrapped around somebody. Unusual. It must have been hard to hold it out like that, but there appeared to be nobody else there.

The woman and the man could not be connected. He was standing at a distance from her. They didn't appear to be talking or linked in any way. He was keeping his distance. Having disabled the surveillance in this area, he would be able to open the doors to let the two people in.

Although he wouldn't question where the information came from, he knew that the woman had to be retrieved safely and concealed in the bunker. She was crucial to what was about to happen.

The man was useful too, he would serve as a cover for James. They would want to know why he didn't follow protocol. James would hand over the man and make him available for BioFiltration. He'd just be a member of the cottage staff who came here when the sirens went off.

Lucky – or unlucky – depending how you looked at it. That would act as a cover for the woman. He'd be able to get her safely in the lift before he distracted everybody in the Control Room with the man's arrival.

She'd be going to a place where they wouldn't find her. Somewhere that he didn't even know existed in the bunker at that time. He'd be guided there via the blue device in his neck.

This woman would soon be able to play out her part in this, under cover and out of sight.

Chapter Fourteen

Deeper

I'm pretty stunned when the lift starts to move downwards. I'm nervous that moving to Level 3 may have alerted Kate and her team in the Control Room. I don't want to get into any more trouble so, rather ridiculously, I press the button for Level 2 again, as if it's going to conceal what I have just done.

I step out into Level 2 and just wait in the corridor. I assume that I'll be joined at any moment by Kate and her security team. They must know what just happened. But nobody comes. I walk up and down the corridor and nip into the loos for something to do. A few minutes later I emerge. Nobody comes. They can't have known what I just did.

I head back for the lift, feeling a little more daring now. I press the button for Level 3. Down it goes again. The doors open. The corridor is similar in size and layout to the ones on Levels 1 and 2, but it is coloured differently and is long and curved, rather than dead straight. There is a thick, red stripe going along each side of the wall. It looks more serious here, I think that the red line leads somewhere.

The doors close, and I decide to try Level 4. I press the button. Once again, I go down a level. The doors open, and this corridor looks different as well. The corridors are black this time, but they still have those thick red stripes running along them. Both corridors are completely silent, there are no bunker staff there. I'm beginning to wonder if the lady was telling the truth earlier. Or to be more precise, if she was telling me what she believed to be the truth. I'm not sure what to do. I feel like somebody who just got away with something they're not supposed to do. I expect to hear alert sirens or something similar. But there are no sounds and nobody comes. Kate and her security team are nowhere to be seen.

Regardless of that, there can only be so long until they realize that I'm not showing up on any of the cameras on Levels 1 or 2. For a moment I feel completely stuck. I'm desperate to explore these two new levels, but I really don't want to get any more negative attention from Kate. Every part of me wants to stay here, but I can't risk getting into any more trouble. Dad, Mum, David and Harriet are relying on me. I'm the only one who can look out for them at the moment. So, I press the button for Level 2 and decide to stick to my original plan.

Rather annoyingly, the lift heads for Level 1. Somebody must have called the lift before I pressed the button. For a place that's so hi-tech, you'd think that they'd be able to sort the lifts out. It turns out to be a lucky break though. The lift arrives at Level 1 and the doors open automatically. A man gets in, presumably the chap who called the lift in the first place. But it's not him who catches my eye. It's the man who's walking intently along the corridor towards the exit who now has my complete attention. I haven't seen him before and he looks just the same as everybody else down here.

Except for one thing that's distinctive. There is one of those faint lights in his neck. It's pulsating furiously, but you'd still have to be looking carefully to notice it. However, there's something very interesting and different about this one. The faint light in this man's neck is glowing blue.

Mission Failure

She had not known Roachie prior to the mission taking place as he was much more experienced in Army life than she was. After completing her basic training, and what seemed to be a very large number of psychometric and aptitude tests, she was summoned to a meeting at a barracks that she'd never heard of before, let alone been to. She called it a barracks, but the soldiers that this place housed wore a uniform that she'd never seen previously, certainly not Army, Navy or Air Force – or even SAS come to that – but definitely military in nature.

You get used to doing what you're told in the Army so she didn't question it when she was asked to sign an E-Notice. She'd already signed the Official Secrets Act as a standard part of her military life, but she'd never had to sign an E-Notice before nor had she ever heard of one. Rather than reading the text thoroughly, she'd skimmed it, just to get a sense of what she was doing. But really, did she have much choice in the matter? She trusted the Army; they had her best interests and the interests of the country at heart, right?

There were sentences referring to 'injections and implants', all pretty standard practice in Army life, where you may get posted anywhere in the world and have to take your 'shots' to protect you from whatever nasties were out there. She'd never seen this before in any of the documents that she'd signed during her short military career. In outlining the types of threat that she might encounter – including via air, sea and land – this E-Notice made mention of 'off world' threats. She just assumed that this was one of those legalese 'cover all' statements. Like 'Acts of God' in the home insurance policy. It's the sort of statement that the lawyers can use to wheedle their way out of anything. 'Could apply to meteorites and bits of fallen space stations, I guess,' she thought, and moved on, without further reading, to the signature area.

Besides, as a young nineteen-year-old hungry for adventure, why wouldn't she be up for this mission? It was an opportunity to play at being James Bond, a bit of espionage. For some reason, she and this other guy had been selected entirely on the basis of their psychometric profiles. A random pairing of no significance, or so it had seemed at the time.

Of course, they had to be trained to a certain level of military competency, but it was their minds that were being sought for this particular job. It was a safe mission, they'd been assured of that from the start. A one percent casualty risk, apparently. Some boffin would have modelled it on a computer somewhere and come up with that figure. In military terms, that risk is fine. In fact, in a simple office risk assessment, that's probably okay. No more than a knocked over hot coffee or a trip over a waste paper bin. Annoying, painful for a short while, but not in need of a hospital visit. With both of them in hospital only forty-eight hours later, one of them on life support, that particular boffin might have wanted to double-check that figure of one percent.

Selection

It had been interesting to hear the objections and concerns that people had when they were going to become a part of a very unique operation. It never failed to fascinate him; human beings are such complex, yet predictable, things. They just wanted to know that their families would be fine and that the outcome would be good. They had been chosen specifically on the basis of detailed psychometric testing. This testing process had been pioneered many years earlier, and had been proven to work time and time again in live simulations. In all respects these were just average people. Of course, they had certain basic parameters of health, fitness and intelligence. But these were not the defining qualities for selection.

Every person selected for service in the bunker had been specially screened to ensure that they would act in exactly the same way in a simulation process. There were key indicators in their personality profiles which ensured that with 99.9 percent accuracy, in moments of stress, they would behave the way that they needed to. And most importantly, they had a predisposition to accept the concept of 'the greater good.' Not everybody got that one. If you had to die to protect a person that you don't know, to do something that would help other people, would you sacrifice your life? Many people say 'no' without hesitation. Others say 'yes' but simulations show that they won't follow through. There is another profile group which would only do so with further qualification and much more information. But in the blink of an eye, faced with sudden and overwhelming information confirming that you must give your life for the good of others, would you do it?

It turned out that you can select a specific group who will say 'yes' without hesitation, because in an instant, they can see the logic of one death to save many lives. It takes a very unique mix of empathy, intelligence, bravery, logic, decision-making … he'd isolated over fifty-seven key factors in this process. But he needed to be sure – with 99.9 percent accuracy – that when these people who'd been gathered in the bunker learned the terrible truth that they would make the right decisions for the greater good. The future of all humanity.

Chapter Fifteen

In The Shadows

This has really got my interest. How come this guy has a blue light in his neck and everybody else that I've seen so far has a red one? Why do I seem to have more access to this bunker than anybody else that I've met here so far? Including Kate. I wouldn't describe myself as unlucky, but neither am I a magnet for massive good fortune. So the thought that I might be the only person on the planet to be able to access virtually all the areas of this secret facility is preposterous. I'm sixteen years old for goodness' sake. I'm still not allowed to buy a pair of scissors, let alone access a top secret military facility.

Something is going on here and I'm becoming increasingly intrigued, the more I learn. I'm desperate to take a look around Levels 3 and 4, but I want to know what this man is up to. He seems very intent, whatever it is, but I reckon that this blue and pulsating light must single him out as being different in some way. Maybe he's a higher rank, or perhaps he has unique access to the entire bunker. Who knows? Anyway I'm going to postpone my visit to the newly discovered levels and see what he's up to first. But not before I do a quick test.

'Excuse me!' I shout to him as the lift doors open to reveal him walking along the corridor.

'I'm trying to get to Level 3 and the lift doesn't appear to be working.'

'Level 3 doesn't exist,' he replies. 'It's there in case they expand the bunker in future.'

'Okay, thank you!' I reply and pretend to head off the other way along the corridor.

Scooby-Doo and Shaggy would be proud of me. I double back and follow at a safe distance along the corridor. Whatever is going on with Levels 3 and 4, the bunker staff certainly believe that they don't exist. Or, they're forbidden to share that information. However, that lady who did the demonstration earlier certainly couldn't operate the lift beyond Level 2. I wonder if this chap with the blue flashing light in his neck could do it. Maybe that's what the colours signify? No time to debate this now though, he's heading at some pace along the corridor.

He seems to be making for the bunker entrance, but that can't make sense, there's nothing to be done out there for now. According to Kate, we have to wait here until we get mission instructions. And then I observe something as I walk quietly behind him in the shadows. Ever since we committed to heading out towards the bunker entrance, I've noticed something different about the surveillance cameras. Beforehand, they were constantly showing signs of life via their whirring lenses and flashing LEDs. But these cameras are lifeless, they don't appear to be powered up.

Whatever this man is up to, it is going on unseen by anybody else in this bunker.

Simulation

They both believed that the entire scenario was for real. They carried out the mission with complete conviction and commitment. In fact, they would never know that it was just a simulation. They were test subjects Zero-97/4 and Zero-98/4.

A series of metrics, measurements and data that would feed into the program and get them towards their 99.9 percent outcome. In actual fact it was 100 percent, but in scientific and data terms, the tiniest margin for error was always left. The 'Act of God' in the home insurance. Wriggle room.

The metrics were so accurate by this stage that he was almost bored with the predictability of the outcome he was about to see played out before his eyes. But then he got the surprise of his life. A jolt out of complacency that was to give him a solution all those years later. He'd just found his 0.01 percent.

A Sudden Noise

The woman and the child sat close together at the left-hand corner of the bunker door. They'd said very little, and mainly the woman had attempted to comfort and reassure the child. It was a strange experience to be next to somebody in such blackness, and with no vision, it was almost obvious to maintain some form of physical contact. At first, they'd just huddled up, but as the darkness became complete, she'd placed her arm over the child's shoulders. If it was Dan, David or Harriet she'd have done it instinctively, so it seemed perfectly normal to do it with this child.

The laptop and Dan's phone were close to hand. Harriet's juice had been discarded in the rush, they were hungry and uncomfortable, but otherwise – other than being confused and concerned about what was going on – they had little choice, but to wait and stay still. Unknown to her at that moment, her eldest son was doing exactly the same thing on the other side of the strong, impenetrable blast doors. Such a short distance between them, yet so far away.

And there was another person close by too, but neither of them were aware of his presence. He was standing in the entrance area, far enough away not to be heard, but still and quiet, waiting with the patience of a man who was accustomed to playing the long game. Yet he had one advantage over them. Because of who he was – and where he came from – he had the benefit of limited vision. Before the darkness dominated, he'd managed to put on a special visor. This was like nothing you'd see anywhere else. From a secret place. A special organization. A visor and breathing aid that would protect him from the power of the darkness until he was able to enter the bunker. For a moment after putting on the visor, he'd silently cursed as his view was completely obscured. A change from Night Vision to Penetration Mode, and the two figures huddled together would become much clearer and sharper. Well, one of them became visible at least, the child could not be seen in the darkness, whichever viewing mode that he used. That's why the child was so important to this project, she was special.

He knew the woman; he'd been with her only days before of course. Driving her to the training facility, returning her to the hospital which they were to use as part of her cover story. She would not recognize him, that memory would be erased via the implant in her neck. Or not so much erased. The brain is a powerful thing. It would be suppressed, as good as being erased as far as the brain is concerned. No, she would not recognize him, he'd be just another face in the crowd, maybe with just a slight inkling of familiarity. But it was this youngster who was troubling him. At first, he'd thought the woman had just ended up with someone who'd headed to the bunker at the same time as her. The first thing he'd noticed was that this person was about the same height as the boy, probably the same kind of age. But as he stood in complete silence in the darkness, he was struck by a sudden and shocking realization. As he thought back to the youngster's face that he'd observed earlier, he grew more sure of himself. He was as certain as he could be that this was the child that he'd been responsible for killing three years earlier.

Chapter Sixteen

Intrigued

Kate had found the boy's presence to be interesting – intriguing even. Initial briefings at the training sessions had indicated that all personnel would gather in the bunker by 15:00 hours at the latest on the designated day. They would not know who they'd be stationed with until the sirens alerted and the bunker doors closed. At that point, all designated staff were to make their way to the Holding Area on Level 1 – and wait – for half an hour. At this stage, there would be a mixture of mission critical staff and the few civilians who were in the bunker, or had made their way down to it, at the time the alarms sounded.

Civilians were not to be given any explanation of what was happening during transmogrification. Once clearance was given to exit the Holding Area, bunker staff were to make themselves known to civilians and accompany them immediately to the MedLab. There they were to be processed for stasis and BioFiltration. There would probably be concern, anxiety and some resistance, but it was important that all civilians were contained. Bunker staff must change into the uniforms provided in the dormitory areas and immediately head to their stations. Different uniforms to mark different roles within the bunker. Standard security checks must be made.

Bunker personnel should await further instructions, but in the meantime, they should familiarize themselves with other personnel, and the bunker facility. Everything would be as per training simulations.

Full mission clarity would be communicated at 20.00 hours on Day 2. Everything, so far, had been exactly according to training and instructions. Excluding that strange twenty-four-hour technical hitch with lighting and some small timing issues during transmogrification, the timescale seemed to have been largely as described. With the exception of this boy. And his family. Kate had expected a few bunker staff from the cottage to be processed for BioFiltration and stasis. That couldn't be avoided without raising any concerns elsewhere. But nobody else was supposed to be in the bunker when the sirens went off. Certainly not full families. It should have been authorized bunker personnel only – and a handful of regular staff from the cottage. This boy had full clearance to Red and Green Zones. He had unlimited access to the bunker.

He was listed on the biometrics database. That was uniquely matched to each individual; you couldn't cheat it or pretend that you were somebody else. There was something unusual about this boy; something that she knew that she'd need to watch. Somehow he was deeply connected with what was about to happen, but she didn't know how. She had no power or ability to block him in any way, because he'd got full clearance to be here. No, it wasn't a coincidence or freak event that led to this boy being in the bunker when the darkness fell. Somebody wanted him there.

Interruption

One thing I know for sure is that this man, whatever he is doing, is heading towards the blast doors that bridge the bunker and the outside world. And the other thing I know for certain is that my mum is outside those doors somewhere. All of a sudden what lies on Levels 3 and 4 doesn't seem quite so important. This man must be going to try and find Mum. So why isn't he with a security team?

When I was retrieved from the long corridor, three people in biohazard suits came out to get me. They were armed too. I'm not sure what resistance they thought I was going to put up, they could have got me to do anything they wanted to at that moment in time. No need to wave a ray gun at me – just lead me to a plate of food. And I'm intrigued by these glowing lights in their necks. They may be something as simple as a monitoring device – or some way of establishing status, rank or bunker access rights. Knowing how and why these bunker people are different may help me to navigate this place better. I'm definitely going to mention it to Kate later.

Still hiding in the shadows, I follow him up the long corridor, until he reaches the blast doors. The darkness outside doesn't penetrate here of course. The lack of light that I had to tolerate in this area earlier was simply the blackness of an underground tunnel with no lighting and no windows. If he's going to open that door, I'm not quite sure what to expect. Kate said that whatever is out there is not hazardous. And it doesn't seem to do anything to me; who knows why that is? Maybe eating too many burgers does give you superpowers after all? But then anybody between the ages of thirteen and eighteen would be safe from this thing. I very much doubt that the world is about to be saved by burger-eating kids.

I decide to move a little further back, just in case. I'm excited though, a chance to move beyond the doors means that I could be reunited with Mum. She'll probably have to go in one of those pod things, but if I can see that Mum is okay, that's one less thing to worry about. The biggest thing as far as I'm concerned.

The man seems to know what he's doing at the blast doors. These people may not know exactly what's going on, and it may be true that they have never operated within this bunker before. What is very obvious though, is that these people have been trained well. They know the layout and the kit very well. Looking at the complexity of the panel that he's just opened, I wouldn't know where to begin.

He presses some buttons at the console to the side of the blast doors. I feel embarrassed for a moment as that's pretty well where I must have taken a pee while I was all alone in the corridor. Nice one, Dan! You take a pee right next to the hidden panel which might have helped your mum find safety inside the bunker. And I hope that nobody was monitoring these cameras at the time, with any luck they were all in the Holding Area while I was answering the call of nature all over what is basically the front door handle.

I stop dwelling on my shame when I see what happens as the man presses the configuration of buttons. What I can only describe as a fluorescent curtain of shimmering green light covers the entire area of the blast doors. It's pretty amazing, actually, I'm stunned at the beauty of what I'm seeing.

The man presses a few more buttons, makes some gestures across another screen, then places his hand on what is quite obviously an identification panel. More biometrics, probably.

The effect of a positive identification is instant. The huge, iron blast doors begin to creak into life. They are starting to move slowly. He's opening the doors to the area where I last saw Mum. The doors are heavy and very slow to move. I can see nothing beyond them. As a small crack appears between the doors, there is just complete blackness outside. The fluorescent curtain, which the man has activated in front of the doors, appears to act as a barrier between what is inside the bunker and what is outside.

That's all very well, but he seems to be getting ready to step outside. Why would he do that if he'll be caught by whatever it is the darkness does to us? He's not even wearing one of those biohazard suits for protection. Maybe that's what the blue device in his neck does; perhaps it protects him from the darkness? My heart is racing now as the tension builds towards me finally being reunited with Mum. As the gap in the bunker doors begins to widen before me, an alert sounds out on the bunker's announcement system. It's Kate's voice and she sounds very serious. More serious than I've heard her before. 'Dan, I need to see you in the Control Room immediately,' she says. 'We've found your mum. It's not good news I'm afraid.'

Split-Second Decision

It's in moments of extreme stress that we find out who we really are. In the comfort of an office or a classroom, we're very happy to discuss what we may – or may not – do in certain hypothetical situations. But until you face that fear, that crisis, that emergency situation, you never know exactly what you'll do. Heroes and cowards are defined in a split second. The mission objective for Zero-97/4 and Zero-98/4 was to enter the facility under the cover of darkness and to retrieve a set of files, which were securely stored there.

They were to be completely unaware of location, so they believed that they were being transported there via military aircraft, but entirely unaware of their final destination. At the beginning and the end of the mission they were placed into an artificially induced sleep, to sustain the deception. Routine security, she understood, and probably why she had to sign that E-Notice document. If they were conscious of the journey duration, they may have been able to guess location, or at the very least, in which continent they were based.

Her nineteen-year-old self was extremely excited by this prospect. Two years spent working in shops, a sudden and compelling ambition to join the Army to get some excitement, and barely out of basic training, she had been selected for this mission. Less than a year ago she'd been adjusting wrinkled dresses on clothes hangers and refunding customers who'd been kidding themselves by buying a size too small. Now she was getting a bit of excitement at last, this is why she'd joined the Army. Once sleep had been artificially induced, the mission began. The man and woman didn't know where they were. As if woken suddenly from sleep, they found themselves outside the base which formed part of their mission briefing. They did not stop to question or hesitate, they recognized what this was and they knew what to do.

They switched on their Stealth-Shields, hi-tech body armour which would enable them to avoid detection. They had five minutes to cut through the wire, stay out of sight, find the office, retrieve the documents. Adrenalin rushed through their bodies as if somebody had just switched on a gushing tap. He took out some cutters, she held the wire with something that flashed when the two things make contact. This was a deadly, electrified fence and the tool she was using rendered it powerless as he created a hole large enough for them both to scramble through.

There were no searchlights in this camp, although it was lit, surveillance was via body heat. A rat scuttled across the courtyard and a blue laser appeared from nowhere and annihilated the creature before it even had time to register what had happened. The man and the woman knew that this was what they must face, their Stealth-Shields would keep them safe from this hazard. All was exactly as it had been outlined in training.

But this simulation was not being run to see how they reacted when faced with a series of predictable events. It was being run to see how they coped in the face of enormous stress, in exceptional circumstances and in situations which they couldn't possibly imagine. The simulation departed from the training. In an instant, the Stealth-Shields deactivated, as if there had been a sudden, massive equipment failure.

The blue lasers started to flash immediately on sensing the body heat, and he escaped by a millimetre as he ducked in behind her through the door of the main office block. As they entered the building, the whole area disorientated, as if somebody had just picked up the entire block of buildings and spun it round. They could hear alert sirens sounding outside, and the approaching footsteps of armed guards. This was not how it was in the briefing. Security was supposed to be automated. Predictable. Beatable.

In an instant they were in panic, confused and dazed by what was going on. Bullets started to fly down the corridor, their adrenalin levels were soaring. They barely knew each other, but they had to become each other's most trusted companion to survive this. She longed momentarily for the safe life that she had left behind. They communicated in single words and hurried gestures. They were trapped and surrounded, with no chance of success in this mission.

The layout was nothing like it was in the briefing; what had happened here? This was all skewed, everything was in the wrong location here and their protective gear wasn't working. Everything that they knew about this mission had suddenly become scrambled. This was where they would surely die.

They entered the room, pushed a filing cabinet

across the door and turned around to look for cover. They were confronted with a bank of screens on which were live feeds of family members. Her mum, playing bingo. His girlfriend, talking to somebody in their corner shop. Her dad, sitting in the car outside the bingo hall, waiting to pick her up. His mum and dad, viewed through their open curtains, watching TV in their lounge. His brother, playing squash with a friend. Instantly familiar scenes, the people they loved most in their lives and a very clear and sudden threat. Each of the people had a targeting graphic projected onto their head.

A quick assessment of the scene indicated that these were live feeds of family members and they appeared to have some form of weaponry aimed at them. A sixth screen that had been blank suddenly lit up. It was a live feed of themselves standing where they were right now. They were under immense pressure, bullets were being fired outside the door, armed guards beginning to hammer outside on the fortified windows and their loved ones seemed to be in imminent danger. They were completely disorientated, under very real threat and their environment had just turned on a knife edge in a matter of seconds. It is in times of massive stress that character is defined. A voice boomed from the speaker. They recognized what was being said, but the voice sounded unearthly, like nothing they had ever heard before.

'You must chose,' it demanded. 'If you are not dead in ten seconds, they will die.' As if to confirm the seriousness of this threat, a laser flashed from a gun that had been concealed in the ceiling, hitting the ground that separated them. Guns were sounding outside, a countdown clock timed the remaining seconds on the screen, the violent sounds of hammering on the windows surrounded them and there on the five screens were the people that they most loved, targeted by a force unknown, but very real.

'You must chose,' demanded the voice once again. 'If you are not dead in five seconds, they will die.' The man and the woman looked at each other and in an instant, without speaking, they knew what they must do. The lasers powered up, they had to choose now, the timer was at three seconds. They raised their guns and simultaneously they shot.

Her bullet hit him in the head. His bullet hit her in the stomach. As they fell to the ground, the laser shot into the spaces that they had occupied a fraction of a second earlier. The targets were removed from the figures on the other five screens, which then closed down.

The targets pictured on the screens went about their lives totally unaware that they were moments away from a sudden and violent death. The first window was broken and the filing cabinet pushed aside as armed guards flooded into the room. The decision had been made.

The two intruders lay in pools of their own blood.

They had just became Doctor Pierce's 0.01 percent.

Chapter Seventeen

Deception

I don't hesitate when I hear Kate's plea for me to

125

head for the Control Room. In spite of what I'm seeing play out before me in front of the blast doors, I know that I must drop everything to respond to this summons. I'm presently not on any surveillance cameras, so I'd better appear pretty quickly or they're going to wonder where I am.

I run along the corridor making sure that I don't draw the attention of the man at the entrance. Whatever he's doing, it will have to remain a secret to me for now. Like so many other things in this place. I check the surveillance cameras and fortunately the first one to be active is just next to the bathroom area.

I sneak through the door quietly, open my trousers and flies, then rush out again, as if I've been in the loo all this time and I'm just rushing out. I make a big deal of fastening my trousers and zip in front of the first active camera. A bit of overacting never did anybody any harm. I don't want that guy in the entrance to be rumbled, whatever it is that he's up to can only benefit Mum. Unless Kate really does have some bad news for me. I'm about to find out, I've taken the lift to Level 2 and I've finally arrived at the Control Room. At Kate's request, I haven't been in here yet, so I'm interested to get a glimpse of this Red Zone area. I half expect the BioMetrics pad not to allow me access, but the doors open and once again I am allowed to enter without challenge.

What an amazing place. The museum-like Control Room of the previous day had been quite comical to me. Old shop mannequins dressed in dusty uniforms had been placed around massive maps on walls, dodgy old equipment and wooden desks which looked as if they'd come out of a Victorian classroom. It's amazing to think in the Cold War bunker that such ridiculous looking technology would have been used in the aftermath of something that had pretty well destroyed the entire world.

But this Control Room is quite remarkable. It's as if somebody has gathered the coolest tech that you could possibly imagine – and even some that it might be a stretch to imagine – and placed it all in this room. Knowing the Government, they'd spend all that money on the equipment and forget to install the Wi-Fi. Throughout the Control Room there are uniformed bunker staff, sitting at brightly lit consoles, performing all manner of complex-looking operations using mainly hand gestures.

Kate is there to meet me and can see the look of obvious awe on my face. 'This is amazing, Kate!' I exclaim, forgetting momentarily why I am here. 'What's the news on Mum?' I ask, recovering from the visual assault of such a mass of wonderful technology.

'Well Dan, we have managed to locate your mother in the area beyond the bunker,' she begins.

'Nothing I don't know already,' I think to myself.

'She was located in the upper area of the cottage,' continues Kate, with a look of complete earnestness.

Okay, now you've got my attention. Last time I saw Mum, she was just outside the bunker doors.

'We have this visual verification, Dan,' she carries on, moving towards a screen to her right. Kate moves the screen in my direction so that I can see it clearly. 'Using special cameras, we are able to see through the darkness into the areas immediately around the bunker,' she explains. 'Your mother is currently in stasis in the cottage above us. She's completely unharmed and her life signs are all normal.'

She has my complete and utter attention now.

'Dan, I'm sorry but your mum will have to stay there until our mission is completed. Once the bunker doors are closed, they must remain that way until clearance is given.'

Now I know that Kate is deceiving me. Whatever that man is doing at the bunker entrance, Kate knows nothing about it. She either believes that the bunker doors can't be opened or she's knowingly lying to me. How do I know that she's lying? Well, the figure pictured on Kate's screen has Mum's face, but is wearing a skirt, fleece and T-shirt. The face is Mum's. But the clothes are not.

Kate has just tried to deceive me with a photo edit. It's very well done, of course. Whoever that is on the floor of the cottage, it's not my mum. But Kate obviously wants me think that it is. Maybe she just wants to stop me worrying. Perhaps it's just not a priority for her. However, she doesn't know what I know.

At this precise moment, the man who should be sitting at the empty workstation right in front of me is in the process of retrieving her from beyond the bunker doors. How do I know? Because on the vacant workstation is a photo of him, his wife and his kids. They look nice, they're all having fun. These people have obviously been allowed to bring mementos with them into this bunker. And next to the photo of his family is something else that must be very important to him. It's a photo of the man I just left in the corridor, youthful and dressed in a military uniform. And standing next to him, much younger and as I've never seen her before is my mum.

Exceptional

This had never happened before. Zero-97/4 and Zero-98/4 had shown themselves to be completely exceptional. But they had ended up with casualties. This was going to cause problems for the program.

She was the one who realized it first. In an exchange that took an instant, she showed him what they would have to do to beat this situation. It was an exceptional and extraordinary action. Any of the test subjects who'd made it this far behaved with complete consistency when faced with enormous, massive and sudden stress. When confronted with imminent violence and the possibility of death, after complete disorientation and a total and immediate change of situation, with terrible and impossible decisions having to be made in a ridiculously short time. 99.9 percent of the test subjects who'd reached this stage did the same thing every time. They made the only decision that you can in these circumstances. 'Kill me' they would say, sometimes both of the test subjects at exactly the same time. The lasers would fire, but the test subjects would be stunned, not killed.

But Zero-97/4 and Zero-98/4 had messed it up completely. Nobody had chosen as they had chosen in that ten seconds of fear, adrenalin and panic. All of the test subjects would be able to act logically, selflessly and unilaterally. Ordinary people, under stress, but doing the right thing. Saving the people they loved most, making the sacrifice that they knew they must. In the face of massively conflicting and confusing information.

But Zero-97/4 and Zero-98/4 had done something so clever that in all the tests that had been carried out, nobody else had even thought of it. Most of them had given themselves up for dead. Zero-97/4 and Zero-98/4 had seen another way out in what they thought were the final ten seconds of their lives. There was no need to accept certain death. They'd seen what the lasers could do, most people thought that was their only option. But it wasn't.

She'd seen it first, and he'd accepted it a moment later. If they shot each other they could potentially buy more time. It was the only way they could give themselves a chance. They would need to make it look good, and of course it would be painful.

We define who we are in moments of greatest stress. And they weren't getting out of this any other way. He was more accustomed to the weaponry. He knew that he would need to shoot somewhere near the stomach, not directly at it, but to the side. Not to kill, not to maim, but to make it look convincing. To buy time, in case they were rescued, in case they could escape in some other way. She was not so accustomed to the weaponry. Basic training had not entailed shooting real people. This was the first time she'd shot into flesh. She had meant to shoot for the shoulder, close enough to make it look like a heart wound with all that blood.

She misfired and shot him in the head. As she fell to the ground in excruciating pain, she knew that she'd probably killed him. As she glided into unconsciousness those were her final thoughts. Neither of them knew that this was just another simulation. The entire exercise had been repeated hundreds of times.

It was so well rehearsed and they were so certain of the outcomes that nobody had ever thought that one of these specially selected candidates would ever shoot each other. In statistical terms it was impossible … or, to be more accurate, completely improbable. There would be massive fallout over this. They'd have to cover it up, make sure she was removed from the Army, placed out of harm's way. It was she who'd triggered the impossible outcome. He was less dangerous to the program, her colluding partner. If he lived through this, he'd be able to stay.

As events unfolded, both of them lived, precisely as they'd gambled when they'd taken that impossible decision to avoid the deadly lasers and to shoot each other. In the impossible scenario in which they'd been placed, they had gambled correctly. They had outwitted certain death, even though that threat was not actually real. In so doing they had caused damage to each other that would never have occurred in any other circumstances. He had received trauma to the brain and would spend many months in hospital, firstly on life support, then in rehabilitation.

He would fully recover and go on to serve in the Army and enjoy a remarkable career, until being made redundant many years later. She would recover too, more quickly than him, but she would carry with her a lasting injury through life as a result of the bullet wound that she received.

At the age of nineteen, she discovered that she would never be able to have her own children as a consequence of the wound that she'd received on that day.

PART THREE: SABOTAGE

Chapter One

Pretence

At least I now know where I stand with Kate. It's hard to condemn somebody who's being so pleasant and reasonable all of the time, but I can see that she is happy to deceive me – to lie to me. She may not be motivated by any ill will on her part, but I know that I can't trust what she says from now on. I decide that the best strategy is to keep up the pretence that she started. I really wish that I'd paid more attention in drama lessons when I was at school, but I do my best to channel my most convincing acting skills.

'Thanks for showing me this, Kate,' I begin, 'and you're sure that she's okay?'

'Absolutely certain, Dan,' she replies. 'Although we haven't been fully briefed yet on the nature of the events outside, we do know that it is benign and that anybody outside this bunker is – very much like your family – in a state of stasis.'

I decide to probe a little further, and put on my 'wide-eyed and inquisitive' look. The face I use with Mum when I want something, but I need to look cute to stand any chance of getting it. She needs to see me as a harmless kid and not a threat. 'How far does this darkness reach, Kate?'

'We believe it to be global, Dan. Certainly that's what our initial briefings in training suggested, but we get the full rundown at 20.00 hours.'

The next sentence seems to be difficult for her to say.

'Of course, you have full authorization to attend that briefing, Dan, and it will be held here, in the

Control Room and on other screens throughout the bunker.'

'I suppose we'll all find out more then,' I reply, and I hesitate about whether I should mention the faint, glowing lights that I've spotted pulsating in the necks of the bunker staff. It's on the tip of my tongue, but I stop myself asking the question.

Kate just lied to me about my mum. I know she doesn't want me here, but at the moment, she's powerless to stop me. For whatever crazy reason, I have authorization to be here. When 20.00 hours comes – or eight o' clock as I prefer to call it – everything may change. It's irrelevant who that person is that I've just been shown on the screen. I suspect that the guy I saw at the bunker entrance may be the quickest way to reunite with Mum. I decide to bypass Kate and try and find out what he was up to at the bunker entrance.

I'm sure he was about to let someone in from outside, and I'm even more certain about that now I know that he and Mum were friends at one time. I'm positive that I've never seen him before, or that photograph, but I wouldn't claim to have tabs on everybody my parents know. We're not big on old photos in our house, I don't think there are even any baby pictures around, most of what we have are recent images on laptop screensavers.

Most importantly, I really want to find out why nobody in the Control Room seems to be aware of what he's doing.

'Kate, I really appreciate the update on Mum and thanks for reassuring me,' I say. I'm getting quite good at this deception technique, even if I do say so myself. 'I know that you can track me on the cameras, is it okay if I go off and do a bit more exploring? There doesn't seem much more that we can do before the briefing.'

Kate is obviously relieved. She thinks that she's fooled me. She's almost grateful that I want to go off on my own and not pry any further.

'I'm pleased that's put your mind at rest, Dan,' she says. 'Feel free to explore any Green Zone areas and don't forget to pop into the canteen if you need any food or drink.' Emphasis on the 'Green Zone'.

'No problem,' I reply. 'See you later, Kate!' I'm spoiled for choice as to where I'm heading next.

I just know that I need to be taking a good look around Levels 3 and 4. I think that I may get a much better idea of what's going on if I can get down there. But my first stop has to be the long corridor that leads to the bunker entrance. I have a feeling that's where I may begin to find some answers without having to wait for this eight o'clock briefing. I'm about to head out of the Control Room when the entire room explodes into life and frantic activity. Red lights flash everywhere and there's a loud, penetrating alarm going off.

It's a full alert. The bunker doors have been breached.

Stillness

The world was waiting, as if it knew that this was only the beginning. Not a creature moved across the entire surface of the Earth. All was still, and even within the darkness, there was no wind, the seas were calm, and nature was at rest. It must have been similar to this at the beginning of time, when there was no life at all.

Only the creatures that now inhabited this planet were sleeping – in biological stasis – living, breathing, sleeping and completely silent.

It was the same for the birds, the insects, the fish – even the ants had ceased work and succumbed to the unstoppable power of this darkness.

Its blackness might suggest that it was a force of evil, something that had been created to annihilate life on this planet. But it was there because Man made it so. It was there because without it, this would become humanity's grave. Its purpose was to breathe new life into this planet, to help it to live again.

Rescue

James carried out the protocols at the bunker doorway as if he had done it many times before, but in reality, this was the first time that he had carried out this operation. A combination of detail-specific and immersive training simulations, and the data that was currently streaming via the blue, pulsating object in his neck, meant that he could carry out a procedure, which he had never done before, with all the proficiency of an expert. Had he not been under the cerebral control of the blue device, he would have felt more emotion at this stage. Certainly, he would have been amazed at the beauty of the shield that he'd just activated at the bunker doors – the only thing that stopped the darkness beyond the doors breaching the entrance to the bunker. He might have even stopped for a moment to wonder who – or what – might have created this incredible technology.

However, he was receiving his directions remotely, and although he was completely aware of what he was doing, it felt to him much like it does when you ride a bicycle: an automatic process and something that happens without you having to think too much about it. All he could think of was to bring back the two people that he'd spotted on his monitor in the Control Room. He knew that he must retrieve them as they would be mission critical. Critical to the mission that he was involved in. Had the device not been controlling his emotional responses, James would have been shocked at what happened next.

It was necessary for the blue device in his neck to inhibit his body's reaction to his current activities. After all, what he was doing at the moment would have created a massive adrenalin rush under normal circumstances. Even though he'd spent much of his life in the military, the nerves and the heightened state of awareness never went away. The person controlling James's actions needed him to quickly and efficiently carry out this operation and powerful emotional responses would not be required. It was a simple task that needed to be completed without detection and, because of the people involved, preferably without full awareness at this stage.

He was expecting two people to step into the corridor, because that's what he'd seen on his monitor screen earlier. He didn't question that the second figure to enter the bunker from beyond the doors was not what he'd actually seen on his screens, he was just intent on recovering two people. As the woman and the child entered the bunker, the blackness beyond the illuminated shield was so dense and complete that they appeared to be materializing out of nowhere, as if stepping out of nothingness.

There was a reason that neither of them had

succumbed to the powerful black force beyond these blast doors, but they would not understand why until much later. The woman and the child were relieved to be in the light again, and their eyes had difficulty adjusting. There was just too much to take in, in that instant.

James moved towards the control panel that he'd operated earlier, to begin the process of closing the bunker doors. He was not expecting a third person to step out of the darkness, so he was not even aware of what was going on just beyond the illuminated shield. A third figure stepped out from the blackness beyond the bunker doors. The woman and her young companion were completely disorientated and still did not have full vision, but this third person had an advantage, his eyes were already accustomed to the light. He had been wearing a device that had enabled him to have full vision during his time beyond the bunker entrance.

This man was used to making quick and ruthless decisions. As he stepped into the light he had a weapon drawn. He would have had time to think this through, he was very familiar with the processes of strategy and planning. He glided quietly behind the man at the control panel and past the woman and her companion, who could still see virtually nothing as their eyes adjusted to so many hours in complete blackness. Undetected, he made his way at speed along the long corridor, as James moved to assist the bunker's two new inhabitants.

As he turned the corner at the end of the corridor, the man pressed a large, red alarm button – one of many that were placed at regular intervals throughout the structure – and immediately the bunker sprung to alert, lights flashed and deafening alarm sirens sounded everywhere. He needed this distraction; it would buy him some time to find a uniform and integrate himself in this place without being noticed. He knew that the three people who he'd just left at the entrance would be safe for now, even though there might be some difficult questions to answer and possibly even a heightened state of security to deal with in the aftermath. But if he'd played this correctly, nobody would even know that he was in the bunker. And that would leave him a free agent to get to the bottom of what was really going on here. Because if the child was still alive, this was much bigger than anybody in this bunker could possibly imagine, himself included.

27 November 1983

It's difficult to determine from the historical articles exactly when governments throughout the world began to publicly acknowledge the universal threats to the environment. Publicly, many countries rejected the claims of the scientists, others didn't even reveal them to their citizens and some were seen to be taking action, although it was never deemed to be enough.

The public did their bit, turning off lights, reducing aerosol use, buying the correct type of fridge and leaving their multicoloured wheelie bins at the end of their drives. But the damage had been done a long time before that. It was never globally acknowledged, of course it wasn't, there would have been mass hysteria, riots and anarchy. And the planet would have died anyway.

We'd taken the steps that were killing our planet a long time ago, many of them we couldn't have even detected with the technology that we had available to us. We were so blissfully ignorant of the extreme damage that we had done.

So on 27 November 1983, a global consortium representing all territories across the Earth's surface signed an agreement that put us on a path to renewal and regeneration. The world continued to function as it does – wars were fought, pacts signed, treaties forged, and everything else that makes up the daily news headlines. But completely unknown to the population on Earth, steps were in place to secure the survival of the planet, an operation that was taking place only at the highest global level of security. It would take more than thirty years to put in place, but when regeneration began, it would start with darkness.

Secret Reunion

Even though she'd left the military not long after that terrible event, she'd still kept in touch with Roachie. Nothing that could be traced of course. After the mission debriefing, they'd been warned – threatened to be more accurate – never to discuss the events that had taken place that day. Naturally, they weren't direct threats. But it was made very clear that this really was top secret stuff. She hadn't even been allowed to visit Roachie. They'd given her regular updates about his progress, made sure that she knew he was okay. But they were forbidden from ever discussing that exercise together.

They were monitored for a while – phones, emails

and meetings – but she'd shown every sign of being relieved that she was away from military operations. She knew in her heart that she was well clear of it all. Not long afterwards she'd met a man called Mike in her civilian life and they'd married very soon after that. They stopped monitoring her after the wedding. They'd wrongly assumed that she'd put it all behind her.

But she knew how to play the waiting game, and when the time was right, six years later, she reached out to Roachie via a disposable mobile phone and a bit of online research. DIY espionage kits now available using your home PC. He was delighted that she'd contacted him again and they met up when he was on leave: on a train, where they would never even think to monitor.

It was a snatched conversation. It started with a hug. She was so sorry for what she'd done to him, but so utterly relieved that he was okay. A hug from him too. And congratulations about the twins. He didn't know about the lasting damage that he'd done to her, but he too was relieved to see her standing there, alive. They'd never really known what had happened that day. They'd thought they were on a routine mission together. They'd even taken a photo of themselves together just before they'd been deployed. It was the one on Roachie's desk in the bunker, though she'd never got a copy as it had been on his camera. Probably best that Mike and the kids never knew. They understood that the mission was a little unusual.

But what had really happened that day? How did they get out? Their gamble had certainly paid off as far as they were concerned, but when they had come round, they'd both been led to believe that they'd been 'extracted'. Rescued in other words. There really wasn't a lot that they could agree on about that day. Only that there were a lot of worried faces around at that time. Somebody had got into serious trouble over their injuries. And it was very clear to her that they couldn't get rid of her quick enough when the redundancy notice came through. It had the air of a cover up, as if somebody would have to do some serious smoothing over.

They were both agreed on one thing though. Whatever the source of that voice that had demanded a response from them, it was like nothing they'd ever heard before. The voice that had compelled them in such a desperate situation to make an impossible choice. It was at once commanding, threatening, urgent … and definitely not of this world.

Chapter Two

Lost

I know straight away that the alarms are connected to whatever I just left going on in the bunker entrance. I wonder what Kate will say if Mum is waiting there – in a different set of clothes to the image that she has just shown me on her screen. Now that would take some explaining! Kate moves instantly. I hadn't considered it before, but she seems to be pretty well in charge of this place. She isn't shouting orders or anything like that, and in fact I've found it pretty hard to detect any hierarchy here so far. But it's fair to say that she knows exactly what's going on, and, as she leaves the Control Room, she is joined – as if it has been rehearsed beforehand – by four armed guards.

Nobody has placed her in charge, but let's put it this way: they're following her. I run along behind, anxious to see what's going on here.

Split Second

The bunker doors were securely shut and the wonderful colours of the protective shield, no longer required, disappeared as fast as they had started. James rushed towards the two figures, who were blinking madly and rubbing their eyes, desperately trying to acclimatize to the light levels inside the bunker.

'Come with me!' said James, his tone suggesting that this was not up for discussion. He grabbed the arm of the woman and as he did so something dropped from her pocket. There was no time to investigate, the alarms were ringing, he must have made a mistake. The bunker staff knew that somebody was here, at the bunker's blast doors, but they did not know who. If they could make it to the end of this corridor, they may have been able to go undetected. At that moment, the blue lights in the necks of the woman and the man stopped pulsating. They were at rest. This part of the mission was completed; they were safely in the bunker.

Whoever was controlling these devices knew that this man and this woman could now avoid detection better on their own, without the assistance of the devices. Their thoughts and memories of what had been taking place in the past half-hour were restored. As the pulsing stopped, recognition dawned on them both at once. 'Roachie!' she exclaimed. 'Amy,' he replied.

This was not unlike a scenario that they'd found themselves in many years previously. A sudden crisis situation. Limited data from which to make fast decisions. Whoever was controlling those blue devices knew that these two were best when they worked together, under conditions of extreme stress, and without interference from the devices in their necks. A unique 0.01 percent of a test sample. They were being left to get on with it on their own. And it didn't matter now that they recognized each other. In fact, that's exactly how it needed to be. For this part of their mission, they would need to rely on their innate skills and judgement. She was slightly ahead of him, just as it had been all those years ago. As partners, they were perfectly in tune in situations such as this. There were few options.

The alarms were sounding. The alert had been raised. This was not necessarily a hostile situation. Very soon, they would be met by security guards of some sort. Hostile or not, it would result in questions and probably, some form of detention. You didn't have alarms unless something serious was going on. Whatever was going on outside, it had something to do with this place. And there was this additional information that only she could digest and he had no knowledge of. Most people would display huge extremities of emotion when confronted with the sight of this child in front of her. The blue device had suppressed that recognition so far, but now there was no doubt about it. But this pair were one of only 0.01 percent; they didn't do what other people would do.

There had been a lot of trouble over what they'd done all those years previously. But that was why they needed to be here. Together, in this bunker, at this time. James had been scheduled to be here already. Amy would have been lured here at the last moment, when events had taken a sudden turn. Over thirty years in the planning, and nobody could have foreseen this. In an instant the decision was made. All those years ago, it was about buying more time, creating a different option, an alternative outcome when it seemed that none were possible.

James knew in that instant that if Amy was here it had to be connected with those events years earlier. This crazy darkness outside, the secrecy, the planning, the military overtones of the entire affair.

Amy realized the same: it must all be connected, but with the child here too, inexplicably, they must have been at the centre of this somehow. Most people would have waited, like rabbits frozen in the headlamps, so much in panic that they couldn't even see what options were available to them. They knew that they had to buy more time for explanation, to figure out what was going on here.

'Sorry Roachie,' Amy said as she took her laptop out of her bag and smacked James firmly on the head.

She didn't notice the phone that had fallen to the ground to her side. She grabbed the child's hand, and they ran for their lives as Roachie slumped bloodied to the ground.

Fallout

He thought that he was going to be taken off the project after the near-fatal injuries, but by the skin of his teeth he had managed to salvage his role. After all, with so much energy and expertise invested already, and with time running out for the planet, this was really no time for an impromptu change of personnel. He was uniquely qualified for this job, above everybody else on the planet, so a bit of collateral damage was easily explained.

The military were furious, calling him incompetent for allowing live rounds of ammunition during the simulations, wanting his head on a plate because their two soldiers had been exposed to so much real danger. They'd been assured that the worst case scenario was a bad headache and temporary unconsciousness from the lasers, which would be set to stun. But with both Zero-97/4 and Zero-98/4 sustaining life-threatening injuries, this was becoming uncomfortable. It didn't take too long for the posturing and temper tantrums to die down and the assertions of rank to cease. Once it had been passed up and down the command chain a few times, it was agreed that the situation should just be 'contained'.

She was to be exited from her military role, with immediate effect. They'd call it redundancy, move her on without a fuss. He would be given the best care and support possible, then allowed to continue his long and exemplary career. For him, that was the course of least resistance; he was a military man, easier to keep him where he was most comfortable, but no more special missions for him. They would be forbidden to communicate and this would be monitored to ensure full compliance. Besides, he had a strong interest in how they'd both performed that day. Results like those could come in useful, he wanted them out of everybody else's sight. But he wanted them where he could see them. He had known about the meeting on the train, he knew that there was a lifelong connection there. Honestly, a disposable mobile phone? It was easily traced back to her. Nobody else knew about their meeting and he certainly had not shared that information.

The research and tests continued, the furore settled down, and he continued at the forefront of the project, working from his base in the UK. A role sanctioned by The Global Consortium. But ultimately controlled by a much higher power.

Chapter Three

Message

By the time Kate and the guards arrive at the entrance, whatever happened here seems to be over. There is no sign of Mum. That is a huge disappointment for me.

However, slumped against the wall with a fresh trickle of blood from a nasty wound on his head is the man I'd been watching only a short time beforehand. The bunker doors are firmly shut, the wonderful blanket of light across the entrance has disappeared, and there is no sign of anybody else.

Kate is taken aback by this. 'James,' she says, 'what happened here?'

It's strange to see her refer to James's name badge on his uniform. Here we are in a hi-tech installation, yet all the people around us are only just getting to know each other and still have to resort to what are effectively supermarket name badges to figure out who they are talking to. As if she is about to ask him where the cabbages are.

James rubs his head melodramatically and gives

the appearance of being dazed. I've seen acting skills like that before. In fact, I'm the master of them!

'I was running a routine inspection of the doors and cameras,' James explains, 'and I think I must have hit my head on the panel here.'

Kate looks uncertain and turns to the security team for guidance, but there doesn't seem to be an awful lot to say here.

'We'd had a problem with the cameras,' James continues. 'I'm sorry, I should have flagged it in the Control Room, I just put it down to routine teething problems.

'At least I managed to sound the alarm to get your attention,' he adds, almost pleadingly.

Kate appears hesitant, but reasonably convinced by this. What he is saying seems unlikely, yet only hours earlier she'd had to send a team to retrieve me from this very area, so it's certainly not impossible that another problem has occurred here. They'd used biohazard suits when they came for me because they didn't know that the area was fully clear from the darkness outside at that stage. I decide to help this James guy out. I can see through his bad acting, and I want to get a chance to talk with him in private.

'Kate, that head wound looks pretty bad, I wonder if he should get that looked at?' I propose.

With nothing else to suggest, Kate nods agreement, then asks one of the security team to check system records to make sure that James's story checks out.

James is escorted away from the area, towards the MedLab, to get the head wound looked at. The security guys make sure that the control panel is secured, then leave the area. I am lurking, and nobody seems to have noticed. I hope that they won't spot what I've just seen hiding away in a shadowy edge of the corridor. It's my phone. Mum has been here. And James is covering something up. As the security team start to head off down the corridor, I grab the phone and tap the screen to force it back into life. The battery is really low. They can power a fluffy pink rabbit with a cymbal for several days in those TV adverts but they still can't make a mobile phone stay charged for any decent length of time.

Fortunately, because we've had no internet in Scotland, all the connectivity was switched off, so I still have a little bit of life left in the phone. There is a new text message waiting for me. Actually, it's a multimedia text message; if it had just been a text, I might not have looked. It has been sent from Dad's phone. I open it up hurriedly, cursing the battery life on my phone. Could he have sent me this when we were separated? Would the text service even work down here? I open up the video. It is Dad. In the background is Doctor Pierce. It has been filmed outside our front door. It was dark outside when this was recorded.

This must have been filmed that night we got the strange knock at the door, when I thought I'd heard Doctor Pierce's voice. It had been Doctor Pierce. I play the video, and Dad's voice comes through the speaker. It's not that long since I'd last seen him, but it feels reassuring to hear his voice. 'Dan, it's Dad,' he begins. I actually laugh at that.

'Er … Dad, I can see you!' I chuckle to myself.

My mood changes when I hear what he has to say. 'Dan, you can see that Doctor Pierce is with me now. He's asked me to film this because it's all going to make sense to you in a couple of days' time.

'First, Dan, you mustn't worry about any of us, we're all going to be fine.

'Doctor Pierce has told me some of what's going to happen when we're in Scotland. I don't like it, but we get to go to the bunker this way, it's best for the family. And Mum needs this.'

His face moves in and out of focus. I can tell that he had been shaking as he recorded the message.

'You need do a couple of things, Dan, and I just want you to trust me with this, okay?'

I hope like hell that my battery holds out.

'Dan, you must get to Level 3 in the bunker. You'll be able to make contact with Doctor Pierce there. He'll explain more, okay?'

I am completely confused, but I keep listening. I know when Dad is being serious, and he is being serious now.

'Dan, there's something special about you that makes you really important in all this. It's about you, it's all about you and …'

Damn phone! The battery dies and the video dies with it.

Concealed

After all these years and after all that worry, concern, doubt and regret, the first thing that she'd done was to whack Roachie on the head with her laptop. They had to buy more time, cause a distraction, find out what was going on. It would need to look convincing, so unfortunately, blood would be required. There's something about the presence of blood that means that no questions are asked. People immediately respond to it, even if it's only a little bit. So when she'd hit Roachie on the head, it had been a calculated move. To give him an alibi, something to distract from what had really been going on here.

She thought that she knew the bunker layout from her visit earlier in the day, so she was a little taken aback by the appearance of the corridor. It had completely transformed from something grey, dark and made of solid concrete to a lighter, cleaner and very hi-tech appearance. No time to ask why. So much was unusual about this day already that nothing surprised her now. Roachie would have some time to figure out a good story. He wasn't unconscious, she knew that. In fact, it shouldn't have hurt him that much. It probably damaged her laptop more than it did his skull. After all, she should know. Roachie's head was made up mostly of metal plates. It was because of her that they'd had to be put there in the first place. A careless shot with a gun years before.

Well, she had no intention of using a gun ever again, but in this case, a laptop would do very nicely. Giving her and the child just enough time to make it to the end of the corridor and conceal themselves before the guards arrived.

Preparation

He was ready for this to play out now. More than twenty years involved in this project. So many tests and so much planning. He'd felt the strain of responsibility many times before. And he'd nearly been removed from the project altogether, after that incident with the botched simulation.

But the future of the entire world rested on the

success of this operation. And it felt to him like the final scene of a play, with all the key characters gathered on the stage. There was the boy, Dan, and his mother. Dan was a sharp kid; he'd have a lot of growing up to do as all of this played out, but he was sure he was up to it. He'd spent a lot of time with the child already, albeit under a pretence.

His mother was an amazing woman, and in spite of all the incredible things that he'd had to do leading these events, he could still take the time to admire a person like her. The wound that she'd sustained in the simulation, the way she'd reacted all those years ago. He admired her all the more for the way that she'd got on with her life afterwards, almost as if it had never happened. But she'd given him an excellent opportunity – a chance that he never thought he'd need all those years ago.

This woman and her son, they didn't know it yet, but they were the key to this entire thing. And as he looked at what was happening in the top level of the bunker from the display on his terminal, he was really going to need a backup plan if the planet was going to get out of this in one piece. Yes, they were his backup plan: the woman and the twins.

Chapter Four

Exploration

I've just noticed a weird thing about this bunker. There are no plug sockets. I know that's an unusual thing to be noticing right now, but really? Surely somebody has to vacuum this corridor. So where are the plugs? I don't have a charging lead with me anyway, but I would really like to see the end of that video message from Dad.

Something strange is happening as well. And I don't just mean this entire darkness, bunker and 'family put to sleep' thing. I mean it's happening to me. Ever since I left that guy, James, at the door, I've been feeling different. It's the opposite of what happened after Nat died. As if the Bluetooth on my phone has just discovered another device. I haven't felt like this since, well, Nat died. I've got so used to living without that sensation of connection over the years, that it feels really unusual to be getting this now. But it feels great, it makes me feel, for want of a better word, complete. This is how I'm supposed to feel all of the time. It must be this place, maybe something to do with the treatment they gave me in the MedLab.

Whatever it is, I'm feeling sharper, more awake and alert than I have since I can remember. I need to take some action – and fast. It must be approaching 20.00 hours, I'd like to make as much progress as I can before that full mission briefing. I have a feeling that things will change around here when that happens. I suspect at the very least there will be much more purpose to what's going on in this bunker.

Although the descent of the darkness has been frightening enough, I've a nasty feeling that it's just the beginning of something much bigger. I'm also very concerned that I'm living on borrowed time at the moment. I still don't understand why I have access to this bunker; it has to be a mistake or an error. Let's face it, where tech is involved, it wouldn't be the first time!

Yet what was it that Dad had said in the video?

Dan, there's something special about you that makes you really important in all this. And why was Doctor Pierce there with him? So many questions, no chance of any answers yet. The next best thing is to do what Dad had said – go to Level 3 – then to catch up with Mum's pal James to see what he can tell me. He should be clear of the MedLab by this stage, and I need to speak with him alone. I need to know if he managed to make contact with Mum. Whatever happened, she wasn't in the entrance area when I returned, so maybe it didn't work out.

I head off down the corridor to make for the lift. There are a few people going in and out of it when I finally arrive, so I wait for it to clear, then make my own way in. I don't want anybody to see me pressing the button for Level 3. That's my little secret for now. The lift descends and the doors open. I'm greeted for the second time by the thick red stripe running along each side of the wall. There is nobody to be seen in this area, no sign of activity. The best course of action seems to be to follow that red line along the curved corridor, to see where it takes me. The layout of this level is completely different to the areas above me.

The upper two levels, although they have been transformed, maintain the essential structure and layout of the original Cold War bunker. So the rooms are the same size and same position, but they've had the most amazing makeover in the world. This level looks as if it has been built and designed separately. Maybe it was added after the initial bunker was built. Perhaps it has been here all the time. It is much bigger than the two upper levels. What is immediately clear to me is that this area is deserted. If there is anybody down here, I can't hear them, that's for sure.

The other big difference on this level is that there are no Green or Red Zone areas. We appear to have moved through the colour palette once again. The areas here are Blue Zone and Purple Zone.

I come to the first of the doorways off this long corridor and place my hand on the entry panel. So far this has worked for me in Green and Red Zones – I'm nervous, but I need to try my luck here too. The door slides open. Incredible. And there are no alarms. Why can I do this? I'm stunned by what I see. This is an underground barracks of some sort. It's meant to house a lot of people, and it's divided into self-contained areas of twelve beds. It's sleeping quarters, bathrooms and showers for a lot of people, maybe a thousand at a rough guess. Twelve beds, four bathrooms, two large shower areas per dozen people. This is no Paradise Hotel. I'd guess this is military if all these people are housed together like this. It's battery farming for humans. There's a sense of waiting in this room – of expectation.

Whatever its intended use, it is not needed right now. I exit this huge area and re-enter the corridor. I make my way to the door opposite. Once again, it opens for me, even though this is marked as a Purple Zone. The door opens. I seem to have complete access to this place. Except for those strangely marked buttons in the lift: they give me a jolt of activity, but they don't actually take me anywhere; they won't activate for me.

If I was surprised by that last room, I'm shocked by this one. It is full of what is quite obviously weaponry. The like of which I've never seen before. This is really hi-tech kit, recognizable for what it is, but not like anything I've ever seen on TV – except in sci-fi films perhaps. And the military uniforms are light and metallic, they look more suitable for use in space than on a battlefield. Once again, there is no sign of activity or usage here. Just a sense that this equipment is being stored. Ready at a moment's notice to be deployed. For something that might happen in the future.

That seems to be all there is on this level: just two very large areas, military in nature I'd say, but presently unused. I'm about to make my way back to the lift, when I notice that there is a final door, right at the end of the long corridor. I half expect it to be a broom cupboard, it's tucked so far out of the way. It's another Purple Zone area. I place my hand on the access pad. The door slides open.

I walk into a massive operations centre, packed with screens, terminals, displays and workstations. It is far more portentous that the one on the floor above me, whatever goes on here, it's the full works. It is powered up, and on the massive screen that is the focus of this room is a computer-generated 3D image of the Earth. At a rough guess I'd say that this is monitoring the spread of the darkness across the planet surface. We appear to be at 96 percent coverage according to the stats on the screen. It's pretty easy to assess what's going on here.

Each of the workstations has a nameplate on it: Jones, Swift, Lucas, Taylor and so on. But it's the raised workstation at the front on this room that particularly catches my attention. This work area has its own zone colour. This time it's Black Zone. There is an access pad on the desk, so I place my hand on it. I think that the workstation is about to leap into life, then it stalls. A bright red laser-like light is released from the pad and it appears to scan my eyes. I blink in surprise at first, then it resets and tries again. This time I keep still and the scan is complete.

The entire workstation is powered up in an instant. Once again I seem to have gained access to a new zone area without any trouble. If this is a technical error, somebody in IT is in for a big dressing down. It's not the tech that draws my attention, even though it is quite astounding stuff. It's the nameplate on this particular workstation that I notice. This must be where the 'boss' sits. It's raised up and has a lot more technical apparatus than any of the other workstations. But it is that name which warrants most attention here. It reads 'Dr Harold Pierce'.

MedLab

James was escorted to the MedLab by the security team and scanned for injuries. The doctor noted the metal plates in his head with great medical interest. 'How did you get those?' she asked, mostly in conversation, because she could see exactly where they'd come from on the medical records, which were currently displaying on her screen.

'It's a long story!' laughed James, and he let her get on with her tests.

'No concussion at least,' the doctor announced. 'I suggest that you rest here until the mission briefing at 20.00 hours and if you're feeling okay by then, you're clear to return to your workstation.'

'No problem,' said James. It was the perfect solution. With clearance to be away from his station, that should give him time to catch up with Amy and find out what was going on. After all these years, why should they have been brought together once again – and in this place? There was no way this could be a coincidence and he needed to find out why, as soon as possible. Especially as they'd both seen equipment like this before. It was very similar to the room where they'd shot each other all those years ago.

Stealth

Although he'd never actually been inside this place, he knew the drill already. With the alarms now sounding throughout the bunker, he'd be able to slip in unnoticed during the confusion that followed.

This bunker was standard procedure for The Consortium, with its Green, Red, Blue, Purple and Black Zones. Green Zone was available to everybody who had biometrics clearance for Consortium buildings. That included him, fortunately, which meant that ducking into one of the first rooms that he encountered resulted in his grabbing a uniform and name badge. Red Zone was management level, he should be able to access those areas too. Nothing too secure at Red Zone level, just MedLab facilities, Control Room areas, Stasis Rooms and some limited weaponry where it was required. Blue was military operations only. He'd had Blue Zone access previously, but it tended to be mission dependent, the sort of access given to serving troops on a particular assignment. Purple Zone was well out of his clearance level – at that stage you were dealing with some serious issues.

If there were Troopers involved, something really nasty was going on. And then there was Black Zone access. He'd never even got a sniff of that, it was security clearance at the very highest rank. Even Global leaders within The Consortium didn't get that. Black Zone access was in the hands of a very small group of designated people in whose charge rested massive power and responsibility. It was probably in those Black Zone areas that the answer to this mystery lay.

He quickly changed into a uniform so that he blended in. He had sufficient access to this place to be able to make his way around without any trouble, but he was going to need to find a way to get into other zone areas. If he could get to the child, it was his guess that that problems would be solved. Instant access to all areas. As he opened the door, he quickly ducked back into the room again to avoid the security team who were escorting the man he'd just seen at the bunker entrance. He'd caught his name badge as they passed: 'James'. Judging from the colour of that man's uniform, he was Control Room staff which meant that there would probably be an unmanned terminal available in that area.

If he could access the internal mainframe, he'd be able to get an idea of where the heart of this place was. Once he'd located and accessed the Black Zone, the chances were that the answers he was seeking would be found there.

Undercover

If anybody had actually been able to monitor the cameras in the long entrance corridor, the bunker would have looked like the most insecure facility that you could possibly imagine. But if nobody is expecting anything to happen, then nobody is looking for it. This was a routine operation, there were no security issues anticipated. It was James who'd marked the perimeters clear, James who'd disabled the cameras, and James who'd opened the bunker door. Nobody else was any the wiser. So Amy and her young companion, following only minutes behind the armed man who'd just sneaked by them at the bunker entrance, managed to exit from the long corridor just in time to avoid Kate and the security team.

It had been a real 'skin of the teeth' moment, though. As they'd reached the end of the corridor, they'd tried to duck into the first door that they came across. Amy had pushed it, tried sliding it and then realized that entry must be given via the pad to the side of the door. At first she pressed it, then she pushed it, then she thumped it. The door didn't open. The sound of footsteps could be heard approaching along the corridor. Her young companion touched the pad and the door slid open.

They got in just in time to avoid a determined-looking Kate and her security team. Amy was desperate to talk to her new companion, but knew that they'd need a plan first. They had to try and blend in, in some way, but everybody else here was dressed in a uniform. They were in civilian clothing; that didn't seem to be a good bet for going unnoticed in this place.

The room they'd entered was a dormitory, so it was lined with beds, small wardrobes and bedside storage tables. Pretty sparse really. It was a good bet that there would be some clothing in here, so she started to search frantically, looking for one of the grey uniforms that James had been wearing. Frustrated, she found an orange uniform first, but that's what the security staff wore. That was perhaps not the best thing for to her to wear right now. More searching and finally success. She found a grey uniform and the sizing was good. She got changed as quickly as she could and turned to the child to see if they'd be lucky enough to find a second uniform. But her young companion had gone.

Chapter Five

Solution

It had taken only a couple of hundred years of industrial activity for humans to destroy the planet. As it would turn out, their consumption of Earth's resources had proven as foolhardy as thinking that you could sail off the edge of the Earth or that the Earth is the centre of the universe. Theories that are easily debunked when you have the tools and knowledge to disprove them. Hilarious when viewed with the benefit of hindsight. So it would be with man's industrial phase on Earth. In centuries to come, scholars would laugh at how men once thought that they could endlessly plunder the Earth's resources with impunity. 'How could they ever have thought that?' they would cry in astonishment.

There was only one solution to rescue this dying planet, and The Consortium knew that it would have to be done.

It was a matter of survival now, the planet had maybe ten years left before the critical point was reached. It couldn't be done without their help, they'd have to accept the only real prospect that was still available.

The Earth was going to have to be saved using very drastic measures. It would require environmental alteration. Carbon dioxide would be removed from the atmosphere. It would be seeded with algae to convert nitrogen, carbon dioxide and water into organic compounds.

Microbial life would be introduced, geophysical and geochemical processes would be implemented. The Earth's geology and planetary biosphere would require complete recalibration.

These processes had once upon a time been proposed for Mars and Venus. Now they were urgently needed on our own planet.

If Earth was to survive this impending catastrophe, it would require something radical and unique. The entire planet was about to be terraformed.

Clarity

Amy was momentarily stunned. Only moments ago, she'd left her companion standing by the door. Now she was on her own. She allowed herself an expletive. Normally, she was very controlled in front of the children, but she was an adult and this situation required a swear word. Her emotions were running furiously, she'd had a lot to take in in a very short amount of time. And she needed to know what had happened to her family – she was desperate to find out if they were okay. Amy made for the door and had her previous lack of success with opening it. First she pressed – as was instinctive – then she pushed, then she remembered how it had opened the first time. She placed her hand on the pad – it opened.

She stepped outside in the corridor, scanned for any other bunker staff in the area, and when the coast was clear, she tried her hand on the door pad again. It wouldn't open. Okay, so you needed special access to get inside rooms, but once inside, you could easily get out again. She'd need to be careful to follow other people into rooms, try to avoid getting caught without access. There was a long list of people that she needed to locate. And she hadn't even worked out yet if there was a problem with her being in the bunker.

She knew enough about military life to understand that it was very unlikely that there would be freedom of movement for civilians, so stealth mode seemed to be the best bet for now. She would need to summon the nerve to walk confidently through the corridors. Any hint of looking furtive or suspicious and they'd be on to her.

Amy walked along the corridor, aware of the surveillance cameras overhead and trying to get a sense of what this place had become since she last walked along here. It was very obvious that some amazing changes had taken place, and whatever was going on outside, the people in this bunker were connected with it all in some way. Everything here had the feel of military efficiency, but this was not the military that she'd known. Here there was no expense spared, the quality, newness and technology used in everything that she saw was beyond her own experience.

She decided to try to pick up a main flow of movement through the bunker and to follow that to the centre. Wherever she ended up, it would probably enable her to glean a little more information at least – and get a feel for what was going on here.

As she moved along the corridor, she became suddenly aware of a person walking quickly behind and gaining on her. They were walking with purpose, at some pace. She wanted to hurry, to run – and even to look back – but she knew she had to stay calm and continue walking at a steady pace. The person caught up with her and grabbed her arm. 'Come with me!'

Glimpse

So Doctor Pierce is connected with all of this in some way. I'd never known his first name – he'd always been 'Doctor Pierce' when I'd encountered him at school – but this has to be the same person, it's just too much of a coincidence. And in the video message from Dad, he'd been with Doctor Pierce at the time. Dad had told me to find Level 3. Well, here I am and this is Doctor Pierce's desk ... but no sign of Doctor Pierce himself. I'm supposed to find out what's going on here. I lay my mobile phone on the desk, might as well get rid of this somewhere safe, it's no use to me right now.

I scan the screens at the workstation, but everything seems to be set on that graphic of the Earth. The darkness appears to be at 98 percent now. Looking at the time, I'm guessing that we get the mission statement at 8.00 p.m., when it reaches 100 percent. That would make sense, but I'm only guessing here. Maybe putting two plus two together and ending up with five. There's nothing more to be done here as far as I can see.

I scan the work area once again: there's no sign of Doctor Pierce, nothing on any of the screens that gives me a clue and no sign even that anybody has been here recently. A dead end. I decide to move back towards the lift to check out Level 4. I have a nasty feeling that I'm not going to be able to gain any ground here, I think I'll have to wait until the briefing at eight o'clock to get some clarity.

As I head towards the lift, I can hear movement beyond the doors. The lift is moving. If I'm not mistaken, that was heading upwards from Level 4. That means somebody else has access to these levels – it could be Doctor Pierce. I call the lift and it arrives at Level 3 swiftly. As I press the button to Level 4, I notice that one of the two buttons that are unusually marked is illuminated. The same as it was when I had tried these mystery buttons earlier. That means somebody else with my access rights has to have been in this lift only moments previously – and they were heading to Level 4. I press the Level 4 button and the lift descends. The doors open. Once again I am confronted with the black corridor with the thick red stripes all along it.

It has an ominous feel about it. I make my way along the corridor and hear a door slide open up ahead. Everything here is Black Zone, the same as Doctor Pierce's work area in the level above. I ignore the other doors that I pass and make directly for the one which I believe has just been used by somebody else.

It's about where the sound of the closing door came from. When I reach it, I can see that it has just been opened, because the light on the entry pad is still illuminated. Whoever it is doesn't seem to be aware that I'm following them. Either that or they're trying to shake me off. I step into the room, this is unlike anything that I've seen so far. It's the usual hi-tech, but it seems to be some kind of transportation area.

There are platforms on which boxed equipment is placed. But this area doesn't seem to be just for transporting equipment, it appears to be used for transporting humans too. At the far end of the room, somebody is standing on one the smaller platforms. They are surrounded by a pulsating orange light, as if some process has already begun. They have their back to me. I can't see if it is Doctor Pierce. I run towards the area, shouting to get this person's attention. I can see that whatever this device is, it is operated in the same way that everything else is here – by a hand pad. The hand pad is activated, whoever is standing in front of me has just started this process. The orange, shimmering light surrounds the person inside and their image is diffused.

I can't tell what this machine – this contraption – is doing, but it seems to be harmless. The person inside it wanted to do this, they are not in pain or anxious about this in any way. They appear to have done this before. I can see that they're about to turn around – they must have heard me now, even though this thing makes an electronic sound, which seems to be getting more shrill as the process continues. I slam my hand on the panel in the hope that it will stop whatever is happening and I will be able to talk to whoever is in there. In the instant that I touch the panel the person inside turns around. Whatever I just did, it failed to stop the process. In fact, it seemed to complete it. The orange shimmering lights disappear along with the person inside them. But not so soon that I don't get a definite glimpse of who was inside. I suspected it from the minute I had walked into that room. My sense of connection has been fully restored.

For the first time in three years, I feel 'locked-in' again; the signal that I've been searching for all this time has finally been re-established. There is absolutely no doubt about it now. Even through the illuminated orange shield, at the moment that they turned to face me, I knew exactly who that person was. They were older, taller and their hair was different. The person who's just used this device is my twin, Nat. It's the sister who I'd seen dying in front of my own eyes three years earlier.

Chapter Six

Reunion

She'd been alarmed by the words 'Come with me!', but in the instant that she heard them, she also recognized the voice that had delivered them. It was James. He guided her into a Green Zone room that had the appearance of a meeting room. There were no cameras in here; they could speak privately and undetected. They hugged as old friends do, but hung on a little tighter, because they'd been through such terrible events together in their past.

'What's going on, James?' Amy asked. She had so many questions that she needed to ask.

'I signed up for this mission because I need the work; I was made redundant last year,' James began. 'It's not like anything I've done since you and I last served together, but I didn't think anything of it – until you arrived. Amy, I can't explain what happened, but I don't really recall going to the bunker entrance to let you in. I just suddenly became aware that you were there. I knew it was you all the time. I saw your face, but I didn't make the connection.'

Amy recognized this. 'James, I've just seen my daughter, Nat. I can't explain it, it had to be her … but she died, three years ago.' She paused, the pain of those events surging back like a bullying emotion, which refused to stop picking on her.

'I lost her, though; we barely had time to speak, but it was the same for me: I discovered her in the car when I went back to get the phone and the laptop. I saw her, but I didn't make that emotional connection. It just didn't register, but the moment my eyes began to focus again after you'd let us into the bunker, I recognized her immediately. She's older and taller, of course. But you don't forget your own daughter.'

These words hung in the air. Neither of them could offer an explanation. As yet, they were unaware of the blue pulsating lights lying dormant beneath their skin. Resting for now, but ready to be activated again if required. 'And my family are in here somewhere – Dan, Mike, Harriet and David, I need to find them,' she continued after a long silence.

'Amy, your family is safe, but you won't be able to see them, I'm afraid.' At least James was able to offer this reassurance. 'All civilians who were caught inside the base have been placed in stasis, for security and safety reasons. They're safe, but they're asleep, the same as everybody outside the bunker. I don't know who's in there, but we can find out pretty easily. I'll bet that's where your family is.'

Amy was relieved to hear this, but still anxious. 'I'm concerned about Dan,' she continued. 'He'd got separated from Mike when the bunker doors closed. He was calling out to me when we got shut outside.'

'What does he look like?' James asked.

'Same height as Nat, jeans, T-shirt, dark hair …' Amy began.

'I think I've seen him,' James interrupted. 'There was a kid in the corridor earlier, suits that description perfectly. Not sure why he was not in stasis like everybody else though.'

Another question that hung in the air. At that moment Amy's eye was attracted by a faint pulse in James's neck.

'You okay, James?' she asked. 'I'm worried I might have hit you too hard with my laptop. Sorry about that. By the way, I take it you knew what I was doing?'

'Yeah, my head does!' he replied. 'I'm fine; why do you ask?'

'You've got a weird vein in your neck, looks like you're under extreme pressure!' She looked more closely. 'That's no vein,' she continued. 'See if you can see it in the glass, it's a dim light under your skin.'

James couldn't see it in his reflection in the glass, but by pressing on the skin in that area, he could definitely feel something below the surface.

'You too!' he replied.

If she hadn't mentioned it first, he would never have noticed. But there was a definite blue colouring beneath the skin on Amy's neck. She could feel it too. Sometimes the mind can make massive, sudden leaps, piecing together random strands of information and cleverly fusing them together.

Amy remembered her earlier uneasiness about apparently having given blood. When she couldn't even remember giving blood in recent years. And the absence of a mark on her arm. She had a strong feeling that these matters were connected in some way, but no idea why. Their conversation was interrupted. The announcement system throughout the bunker was summoning all personnel to the Control Room.

The Second Genesis

It was 20.00 hours. An alert sounded throughout the bunker. All personnel were to gather in the Control Room or the canteen, depending on their role in these events. In each meeting area, there was a large screen displaying a fixed image and a logo derived from a design of Earth. The same logo that was displayed on the uniforms of every person in this bunker. It had the words 'The Global Consortium' beneath it.

The bunker staff gathered in the designated areas, an air of expectation crackling like an electric current through the building. What happened next would define the mission in precise detail. The holding image faded out, and a man appeared on the screen. It was Doctor Pierce. The chatter in the room died to a hush. The same logo and wording was displayed on the plain background behind Doctor Pierce. He drew breath and began to speak.

'My name is Doctor Harold Pierce. I have met all of you already, but due to the highly confidential nature of this mission, none of you will remember those meetings,' he began.

'Firstly, let me start by reassuring you that your loved ones are all completely safe and secure.'

Nobody uttered a word, but you could feel the collective sigh of relief across the room.

These people were voluntary participants in this

mission, but their contracts stipulated that they could designate family and friends for dedicated support. Basically, The Global Consortium had made sure that they were all in a safe and secure place at the time the darkness had begun to fall. A letter here, a phone call there, the occasional email, and it was easily orchestrated. Doctor Pierce continued to speak.

'The terraforming process that is occurring outside is completely benign to living creatures, though to enable it to operate effectively, it is necessary to place everything into a state of stasis. This will last in total for a period of fourteen days. During this time, oxygen, water, and nutrients will be delivered via TerraLevel 1. This is the process that is connected with the darkness beyond the bunker – that has just reached 100 percent of successful completion.'

Doctor Pierce had a riveted audience, hanging on to every word and scrap of information that he was offering.

'Ladies and gentlemen, while the whole world sleeps outside, you are its guardian for the next fourteen days,' he carried on. 'This process will be fully automated, it is completely pre-defined.

'I must apologize for the initial delays in timing and restoration of lighting. We are investigating the cause of these at present, but we believe them to be routine issues.

'Your role in this is to keep watch over the planet. If your intervention is required at any stage, you will receive further instructions, as per your training.'

He paused, not for dramatic effect, but to gear up to what was possibly the most worrying part of his speech. 'And so to the reason for this mission,' he began. 'The entire planet and atmosphere which sustains it has long been in critical danger. In short, our planet can sustain life in its existing form for no more than ten years. The Global Consortium has made a radical intervention.

'What will occur over the next fourteen days are the essential components required for the reanimation of our planet and its atmosphere.

'The process will continue well beyond the fourteen days, but it will remain undetectable by all available instrumentation. After the project, your memories will be erased of these events.

'The Global Consortium will maintain that recent catastrophes were caused by a series of unexpected solar flares, and although there will be some inevitable casualties, the safety and security of the planet will be assured for many millennia in the future … if we don't continue and repeat the mistakes of the past.

'As military personnel, you will understand the risks involved in a mission of this scale and the overriding importance of achieving the final objective.

'Your individual briefings will be delivered directly to your personal E-Pads. In the meantime, The Global Consortium thanks you for your service in the Genesis 2 project.'

With those final words, his face disappeared from the screen and the holding image returned. Genesis 2 was underway.

Encryption

Seated at James's vacant workstation, he had quickly managed to navigate the terminal. This was a standard Consortium configuration; he had access, of course, via his own work.

Although only on the periphery of this project, he was party to the basics of the Genesis 2 operation. After all, it was he who had escorted many of these people to the training centre and returned them to their civilian lives, all memories erased. He had never met Doctor Pierce personally, but he received his instructions from him via his E-Pad and, of course, he was the very reason he had come to this place: to find out Doctor Pierce's connection with the child. He had basic clearance on the mainframe.

His presence here wouldn't be flagged either, so long as he didn't draw attention to himself by trying to access unauthorized areas. He could see too that since the mission briefing, the entire operation had been stepped up a notch. Security, monitoring, and surveillance were now significantly increased. TerraLevel 2 was about to begin. Although it was fully automated, it would be monitored around the clock. As Doctor Pierce had said, they were guardians of the entire planet, similar to parents watching over children as they sleep. He needed to locate the doctor and confront him about the girl. He also wanted to know how this family was connected. Years of work in this field gave him highly tuned senses for this type of operation.

And he smelled a rat. It was only because he was trying to locate the source of Doctor Pierce's broadcast that he stumbled upon the information that nobody else had thought to check for. He was unable to determine the location of the broadcast but he was sure that it was delivered live and that it had not emanated from within this bunker. Certainly it wasn't on the same mainframe that the Control Room team were using. It was while he was scanning the source that he noticed an unusual thing.

Two video streams were being served simultaneously. The one that they were all watching was shielding something else, which was heavily encrypted. It was a Trojan Horse system used rarely in Consortium circles, but highly undetectable – mainly because nobody ever looked for it. Hiding in plain sight. Somebody, within this bunker, had just received an encrypted message from Doctor Pierce. A message that he didn't want anybody else to see.

Terraforming

The terraforming process was a slow one; these environmental ailments could not be cured instantly. It would take fourteen days for Genesis 2 to breathe new life into the planet. It's said that it took God seven days to create the Earth. Such a work of art is not so easily recreated. First, all life forms had to be put to sleep. This regeneration would take place around them and unknown to them. The darkness that surrounded the Earth would provide everything that the planet needed to survive.

Over the next fourteen days and nights, that black, impenetrable blanket would change colour and begin to lighten as the complex atmospheric, chemical, geological and biological transformations took place.

Even God would be in awe of this process and might be forgiven for questioning how Man had become so advanced that he was capable of mimicking the power of the Creator.

The terraforming process was complex, and it could be used to breathe new life into extinguished planets, or light the flame of first life in dead planets.

It could also be deployed for destructive and selfish outcomes. When God used His powers to create the Earth, it was for benevolent purposes, to give Man the opportunity to live in His beautiful garden.

Imagine, then, if those powers were used for evil and just how much devastation could be unleashed across the surface of the planet if they were.

Contact

It was Nat that I'd seen with Mum! Now I am certain. I don't know what to think or feel. We've grieved for Nat for three years. I've missed her every single day since then. And yet there she was, right in front of me. In the middle of whatever is going on in this bunker. I feel incredibly level-headed considering what's just happened, and I know that Nat and I must be reunited as soon as possible. The fact that she's alive has to be connected with the amazing technology in this place; we must be caught up in all of this in some way.

But how? Nat seems to be able to move around this place the same as I can. And if she's inside the bunker now, Mum must be here somewhere too. I've got to figure out how to get her back from wherever this device took her. And I hope she's trying to figure out how to get back to me; she had just enough time to see me. I hope she recognized me. Since she disappeared moments ago, I've lost that feeling of 'connection' again. It's already dawned on me that this must be hooked into Nat, it must be a 'twin thing'. Useful though, because I seem to be able to sense when she's around.

I must have been picking up on her ever since she managed to get through the bunker doors. If she's definitely below ground now, that timing seems about right. At that moment, an announcement and alert sounds through the transportation area and the corridors outside. It is eight o'clock, the time of the mission briefing. I curse what's just happened with Nat and the fact that I've got caught here, on Level 4, at the time of the briefing.

I need to run by the Operations Centre on the floor above. I left my phone on the workstation there and I want to ask Kate how I can charge it. I want to see the end of Dad's video too, it might tell me how I can reconnect with Nat.

I rush back to the lift, and return to the third level. The announcement that the briefing is about to begin is sounding throughout both of these lower levels, which nobody else seems able to access, so far. They must all be connected in some way if they share the same announcement system. I head back to the Level 3 Operations Centre and make straight for Doctor Pierce's console. I pick up my phone and it lights up as my hand touches the screen. I check the battery life as it should be dead. It's fully charged now. How did that happen?

This bunker must have wireless electricity. That would explain the lack of plug sockets. I wonder if that's how it works, this place is certainly techie enough. I'm about to open up the MMS message that Dad sent me, when a familiar face appears on every single terminal in the room. It's Doctor Pierce. He begins to speak: 'My name is Doctor Harold Pierce, I have met all of you already, but due to the highly confidential nature of this mission …'

His words are cut off on the terminal at this workstation. On all other terminals he is delivering a briefing speech: 'Firstly, let me start by reassuring you that your loved ones are all completely safe and secure,' he goes on. But on the screen I'm looking at, he's saying something very different. It's an overlaid message, as if one message is embedded within another.

'Dan,' he begins in the second message. 'This is an encrypted update, which only you will be able to receive.'

'At present, you are the only person in the bunker who has Purple or Black Zone access. That won't be the case for much longer. I don't have much time to speak, we're currently on an encrypted delivery system. You'll have worked out already, Dan, that you and your sister are very special.'

I begin to talk, but he continues to speak over me. This can't be a live message; he must have recorded it beforehand.

'Dan, as you'll see on the main screens, I am currently explaining to the bunker personnel what's going on outside. I don't know if you've ever heard about terraforming, but we're involved in the highest level project to regenerate the planet.

'That automated process will begin the second my mission briefing ends. Bunker personnel will receive their agendas directly to their personal devices.

'Dan, I've spent more than twenty years personally preparing for this. I thought I'd covered every possibility, but I've missed something … I can't believe I didn't see it.'

I get the feeling that he isn't here to deliver good news to me.

'The terraforming has been hijacked by a terrorist faction, Dan. I don't know who they are – or where they are – I just don't understand how they even got access, it should be impossible, it's all tied into me.'

He's flustered and has the look of a genius who's just been told that his theory is rubbish, even though he knows that it must be correct.

'If they sabotage the terraforming, Dan, they can kill the planet ... everything will be dead. It's the minerals they want – and the gas – they don't care about what else is left.'

He's getting quite distressed now. I'm with him on that.

'I managed to get some people inside the bunker who you can trust, Dan – your mum is one of them, and James, her friend. You can tell if they're safe by the devices in their necks.

'Look closely under their skin; you should see a very faint, blue, pulsating light there. If you do, they're safe, they're connected directly with me.'

He furrows his brow. 'If they have any other colour device, Dan, you mustn't trust them. I have partial control, but the encryptions were hacked when the sirens sounded. It's why the lights were off in the bunker for so long, why the timing was all wrong. They hacked in when we were at our most vulnerable – as we handed over from governmental control to the bunker.

'Dan, I've got to go. Remember, you can access all areas here, but you've only got a short head start on them. Once the hacking is complete, they'll have the run of the place.

'One last thing, Dan: they'll go for the terraforming last of all. First thing they'll target are the drones.'

The message ended. Just as his final words were delivered on the second presentation that had been continuing on the main screens.

'... The Global Consortium thanks you for your service in the Genesis 2 project.'

Chapter Seven

20.05 Control

At the very moment that Doctor Pierce finishes his briefing in the Control Room, Amy notices something that she might have missed if it wasn't for her conversation with James only minutes before. In unison, the minute the screens return to The Global Consortium logo, the necks of the bunker staff glow red. She turns to James. His neck is fine, still blue.

He notices what just happened too, and reads her face when she nudges him. 'You're fine!' he acknowledges, checking out her neck. The light is blue.'

Across the room there is a simultaneous *beep* as the bunker staff receive their instructions on their personal devices, just as Doctor Pierce had suggested. There is a sudden air of purpose, as Control Room staff access their personal mission agendas. The time for acclimatization is over; Genesis 2 has begun.

'I need to get back to my station,' James whispers, 'I'll find out what I can.'

He walks towards the man who had taken up his duties in his absence, somebody he hasn't noticed here before. The man makes way for him, and seems lost momentarily, he has no place to go. He is saved by the alarms that began to sound on a console to his left.

'Stasis Room power has been cut, as requested,' the terminal operator reports to Kate.

'How long?' asks Kate.

'A maximum of one hour independent survival for the adults, about forty minutes for the children.'

Amy hears everything.

James walks over to her and whispers hurriedly. 'They're killing the civilians in the Stasis Room, Amy: they've turned off the power supply. Take my E-Pad, I've mapped in the location. When you get there, I'll send instructions to work around it without detection. I'll do what I can here while you're on your way.'

Amy leaves the Control Room, adrenalin flowing, heart beating furiously. Unknown to her, the man who had been sitting at James's terminal notices her departure and follows her, making sure that he is not detected. She is suddenly aware of a feeling that she hasn't experienced in some time, since those terrible events with James. It is survival instinct. She follows the navigation data on the E-Pad and manages to make her way through the corridors easily enough. James must be monitoring on the cameras. As she approaches the Stasis Room door, it slides open without her having to place her hand on the panel.

James is good, he must have managed to override it. Unfortunately, his actions are detected immediately by Kate. Security just went up to maximum level and anything that is out of the ordinary now gets relayed to her instantly. Inside the Stasis Room, it doesn't take Amy long to work out what is happening.

Encased in glass cocoons, she finds her family and other people, some of whom she recognizes as the bunker staff that she'd seen on the previous day. To the side of each of the inanimate bodies is a life-signs indicator. The levels on the graphs are going down, bit by bit. Heart rates are slowing. These people are dying. She has to save her family. The Stasis Room door opens.

With the blue device in her neck currently inoperative, she recognizes him straight away, but she can't place where they have met before. The alarms are sounding in the corridor outside, they must have spotted her. The man in the doorway looks as if he is about to speak, but becomes aware that there are heavy footsteps behind him. A security team is following just behind. He takes the gun that he has been hiding within his uniform, points it at Amy, and shoots. She falls to the ground.

As the security team enters the Stasis Room, a small pool of blood has begun to form where her body lies still and lifeless.

20.14 Drones

Kate receives the news that the intruder in the Stasis Room has been dealt with. Unknown to the man called James, she alerts Security to his recent unsanctioned actions. Combined with his unexplained visit to the bunker entrance earlier, he obviously means trouble. They catch him unawares as the security team storms quietly, but efficiently into the Control Room and take him away for interrogation.

With the red devices pulsating furiously in their necks, interrogation will now mean something completely different to what it did only an hour previously. Somebody else is now calling the shots here; internal sabotage will neither go unnoticed nor unpunished. Kate continues to work through the tasks that are being directly transmitted via the device in her neck. By a source unknown.

As the faint red glow pulsates, she executes her next task with no emotion or any thought of consequence.

'Begin drone activation!' she commands as the woman in front of her, responsible for carrying out that task, sets to work at her console.

'Activation sequence has begun, authentication required to process,' the woman replies.

Kate places her hand on a panel at her desk. Her eyes are scanned by a red laser. This is a Black Zone security operation. Kate now has top level access.

'Drone activation underway!' comes the confirmation from across the Control Room. 'Initiating the arming sequence!'

20.16 Peril

My mind is racing. First, Nat's reappearance – or should I say 'resurrection'? Now this message from Doctor Pierce. Dad said to trust him. Doctor Pierce said to trust Mum and James. I need to start tracking people down – and fast! I remember the unfinished video message on my phone, and begin to replay it. I get to the part where it broke off earlier: 'It's about you, it's all about you and …'

The message continues: '… It's about you, it's all about you and Nat. It's because you're twins, it's all about you two. Dan … Nat is alive. It's all connected with your genetic patterns, you have to work together. Doctor Pierce says I'm not going to remember recording this afterwards, so it's in your hands, Dan. Trust Mum, look for Nat, and do everything together.'

As he said that last word, I could see Doctor Pierce operating some electronic device behind him. His expression turns blank and I hear Doctor Pierce's voice say, 'Now go back inside,' as the video comes to an abrupt end.

'Work together'. Everything that won't work for me in this bunker seems to need something else. Or someone else. The weird buttons in the lift. There are two of them. When Nat was in that machine earlier, as soon as I placed my hand on the pad to try and stop it, it seemed to do the opposite – it actually completed the process. I need to get back to that transportation room where I left Nat.

I run as fast as I can, back to the area where Nat disappeared. The activation panel is illuminated. Nat must have touched it already. I place my hand on it once again and the vibrant orange light surges into life.

End

Moments after Dan leaves the Operations Centre, one by one, three of the large screens flicker into life. On one is the face of a woman. There are men's faces on the other two screens. Each of them looks serious, grave, concerned. Behind them are control rooms, exact replicas of the one only two floors above. Each of the people on the screens is attempting to deliver an urgent message. A message that goes unheard: 'Quadrant 2 to Quadrant 1, breaking communication protocols to transmit this urgent message. We're receiving data that indicates armed drones are being activated in your Quadrant. This is a Tier 10 alert … they're targeting the remaining three bunkers!'

As the urgent message is broadcast to the empty room, two levels up a woman lies bleeding in the Stasis Room. Shot by a man who is being congratulated by the security team at this very moment. The only man who can help her is being escorted under heavily armed guard to an interrogation room. A room which he is unlikely to exit alive. Around her are the dying bodies of her family, deprived of life by the glass coffins which were meant to protect them.

In the Control Room on the floor below, a woman named Kate has just given the instruction to arm hundreds of drones. Their targets are the other three bunkers which have been secretly built to act as joint guardians of the Earth while the terraforming takes place. The Earth is in peril; its cries for help go unheard. But on the lowest level of this bunker a sixteen-year-old boy has just placed his hand on a panel.

The machine whirs into life, recognizing his genetic pattern. Bright orange lights circle the platform and a figure appears as if from nowhere. It is a girl, about sixteen years old, and she knows the boy. She steps off the platform and grabs him urgently by the hand. It is the first time they have been together since they were violently parted three years ago.

'Come with me!' she says. 'I've figured out how to stop this!'

Preview of The Secret Bunker Trilogy, Part 2: The Four Quadrants

Targeted

This floor is bigger than all the rest. It must be the size of twenty football pitches, it is a vast sub-terrestrial hangar. There will be one of these in each of the bunkers, the underground control centres which form the four Quadrants of The Global Consortium.

The drones are like nothing he's ever seen before. They're smaller than the military versions that he watched in awe on the TV news programmes, but they look immediately more sinister and deadly. There are hundreds of them here, like bats in a cave, still and silent.

In an instant, the drones activate, one after the other. Red lights, the eyes of a devil, illuminate in the darkness. When all of the drones appear to be triggered, a bright shield of light sweeps across the full width of the far wall. It is a sight to behold and in any other circumstances it would be considered a spectacle of great visual beauty.

There is a deep rumble at the far side of the hangar and slowly, surely and deliberately its vast iron sides open up to reveal a dense blackness beyond. The drones launch into the darkness outside and as they enter that bleak nothingness they appear to have been swallowed up by some malevolent force. But it is not the darkness itself that is evil, it is the drones which make their deadly journeys within it.

Unseen by any human eye, they launch at regular intervals, each with a terrible mission. The red lights on the drones are not the eyes of a devil, though they may just as well be. Instead they indicate that the devices are armed, they have become a powerful weapon of destruction. Each one is intent on its deadly assignment – to completely annihilate the other three bunkers which lie beyond in the remaining Quadrants.

Lab Rat

The girl is restrained on a cold, metal operating table. She is no more than sixteen years of age. Unable to move even her fingers, let alone her arms, legs or head, she has been like this for over twenty-four hours now, given neither food nor water. Four small needles have been inserted at angles into the base of her spine. Once every hour for the past twenty-four hours a mechanized delivery system has injected four different liquids directly into her spinal cord.

She hasn't been told why she's here or why they have chosen her for these experiments. There are no others like her, she is all alone in this nightmare. Another hour is up. The machine whirs into life once again, and the serums are injected into her one by one. It is the final liquid which she dreads most, the one that results in agonizing spasms which last nearly the full hour until the next injection is administered.

She lets out a scream of pain which echoes down an empty corridor. The only person who's aware of what is going on here is the man who sits at his desk diligently monitoring the results of this experiment.

His office is plain and undecorated, there are no family photographs or pictures on the walls here. The only sign of who is he is and what he might be are displayed on the badge which is attached to his white lab coat. It reads 'Dr H. Pierce'.

Awoken

It was never intended that this fighting force should ever see the light of day. Specially selected more than eighteen years earlier, they'd been chosen as part of a series of initial experiments specifically for this purpose.

Tested under the most extreme conditions, each cryogenically frozen body in this room had been included on the basis of consistent responses in a series of demanding simulations. Unknown to them, they had been frozen here since the tests ended, waiting for the time when their unique services might be required. That time was now.

The entire population of the Earth was in imminent danger from terrorist saboteurs, their evil ambition to extinguish all life on the planet and extract its rich mineral deposits for sale to the highest bidder. As the power surged through their cryogenic caskets and the blood began to flow once more through their male and female bodies, the awakening cohorts could never have guessed at the battle that lay before them. It would be a battle not only to preserve their own lives, but also to protect the lives of every remaining human being on the planet.

Read The Secret Bunker Trilogy, Part 2: The Four Quadrants

More details via The Secret Bunker Trilogy website at http://thesecretbunker.net

PAUL TEAGUE

PLEASE LEAVE A REVIEW

If you enjoyed The Secret Bunker: Darkness Falls
please leave a review on Amazon to help more
readers to discover the trilogy – thank you!

http://thesecretbunker.net/review

ABOUT THE AUTHOR

Paul Teague has worked as a waiter, a shopkeeper, a primary school teacher, a disc jockey and a radio journalist and broadcaster for the BBC. He wrote his first book at the age of nine years old. The handwritten story received the inevitable rejection slip, but that did not stop him dabbling with writing throughout his life. 'The Secret Bunker' was inspired by a family visit to Scotland's Secret Bunker at Troywood in Fife, Scotland, and is Paul's first full-length story.

17398932R00107

Printed in Great Britain
by Amazon